He was coming unglued.

She knew it, knew that it would be like this.

Knew the second she had seen the tall, dark, brooding doctor, and heard his voice.

Knew that there was trapped emotion within him that if she could only tap, would sweep her away.

And she needed to be swept away, needed to feel, just for a moment, as if every star in the universe was in the right place and that everything, *everything* would be all right.

Anything less was unthinkable.

Dear Reader,

It's hard to believe that it's *that* time of year again—and what better way to escape the holiday hysteria than with a good book…or six! Our selections begin with Allison Leigh's *The Truth About the Tycoon,* as a man bent on revenge finds his plans have hit a snag—in the form of the beautiful sister of the man he's out to get.

THE PARKS EMPIRE concludes its six-book run with *The Homecoming* by Gina Wilkins, in which Walter Parks's daughter tries to free her mother from the clutches of her unscrupulous father. Too bad the handsome detective working for her dad is hot on her trail! *The M.D.'s Surprise Family* by Marie Ferrarella is another in her popular miniseries THE BACHELORS OF BLAIR MEMORIAL. This time, a lonely woman looking for a doctor to save her little brother finds both a healer of bodies and of hearts in the handsome neurosurgeon who comes highly recommended. In *A Kiss in the Moonlight,* another in Laurie Paige's SEVEN DEVILS miniseries, a woman can't resist her attraction to the man she let get away—because guilt was pulling her in another direction. But now he's back in her sights—soon to be in her clutches? In Karen Rose Smith's *Which Child Is Mine?* a woman is torn between the child she gave birth to and the one she's been raising. And the only way out seems to be to marry the man who fathered her "daughter." Last, a man decides to reclaim everything he's always wanted, in the form of his biological daughters, and their mother, in Sharon De Vita's *Rightfully His.*

Here's hoping every one of your holiday wishes comes true, and we look forward to celebrating the New Year with you.

All the best,

Gail Chasan
Senior Editor

MARIE FERRARELLA

The M.D.'s Surprise Family

Silhouette®
SPECIAL EDITION®
Published by Silhouette Books
America's Publisher of Contemporary Romance

To Gail Chasan,
with thanks and delight

SILHOUETTE BOOKS

ISBN 0-373-24653-6

THE M.D.'S SURPRISE FAMILY

This edition published by arrangement with Harlequin Books S.A.

Visit Silhouette Books at www.eHarlequin.com

Printed in U.S.A.

Books by Marie Ferrarella in Miniseries

ChildFinders, Inc.
A Hero for All Seasons IM #932
A Forever Kind of Hero IM #943
Hero in the Nick of Time IM #956
Hero for Hire IM #1042
An Uncommon Hero Silhouette Books
A Hero in Her Eyes IM #1059
Heart of a Hero IM #1105

Baby's Choice
Caution: Baby Ahead SR #1007
Mother on the Wing SR #1026
Baby Times Two SR #1037

The Baby of the Month Club
Baby's First Christmas SE #997
Happy New Year—Baby! IM #686
The 7lb., 2oz. Valentine Yours Truly
Husband: Optional SD #988
Do You Take This Child? SR #1145
Detective Dad World's Most Eligible Bachelors
The Once and Future Father IM #1017
In the Family Way Silhouette Books
Baby Talk Silhouette Books
An Abundance of Babies SE #1422

Like Mother, Like Daughter
One Plus One Makes Marriage SR #1328
Never Too Late for Love SR #1351

The Bachelors of Blair Memorial
In Graywolf's Hands IM #1155
M.D. Most Wanted IM #1167
Mac's Bedside Manner SE #1492
Undercover M.D. IM #1191
The M.D.'s Surprise Family. SE #1653

Two Halves of a Whole
The Baby Came C.O.D. SR #1264
Desperately Seeking Twin Yours Truly

***The Reeds**
Callaghan's Way IM #601
Serena McKee's Back in Town IM #808

*Unflashed series

Those Sinclairs
Holding Out for a Hero IM #496
Heroes Great and Small IM #501
Christmas Every Day IM #538
Caitlin's Guardian Angel IM #661

The Cutlers of the Shady Lady Ranch
(Yours Truly titles)
Fiona and the Sexy Stranger
Cowboys Are for Loving
Will and the Headstrong Female
The Law and Ginny Marlow
A Match for Morgan
A Triple Threat to Bachelorhood SR #1564

***McClellans & Marinos**
Man Trouble SR #815
The Taming of the Teen SR #839
Babies on His Mind SR #920
The Baby beneath the Mistletoe SR #1408

***The Alaskans**
Wife in the Mail SE #1217
Stand-In Mom SE #1294
Found: His Perfect Wife SE #1310
The M.D. Meets His Match SE #1401
Lily and the Lawman SE #1467
The Bride Wore Blue Jeans SE #1565

***The Pendletons**
Baby in the Middle SE #892
Husband: Some Assembly Required SE #931

The Mom Squad
A Billionaire and a Baby SE #1528
A Bachelor and a Baby SD #1503
The Baby Mission IM #1220
Beauty and the Baby SR #1668

Cavanaugh Justice
Racing Against Time IM #1249
Crime and Passion IM #1256
Internal Affair Silhouette Books
Dangerous Games IM #1274
The Strong Silent Type SE #1613
Cavanaugh's Woman SE #1617
In Broad Daylight IM #1315
Alone in the Dark IM #1327

MARIE FERRARELLA

This RITA® Award-winning author has written over one hundred and twenty books for Silhouette, some under the name Marie Nicole. Her romances are beloved by fans worldwide.

What's Happening to the Bachelors of Blair Memorial?

Bachelor #1: Lukas Graywolf + Lydia Wakefield =
Together Forever IN GRAYWOLF'S HANDS (SIM #1155)

Bachelor #2: Dr. Reese Bendenetti + London Merriweather =
True Love M.D. MOST WANTED (SIM #1167)

Bachelor #3: Dr. Harrison MacKenzie + Nurse
Jolene DeLuca = Matrimonial Bliss MAC'S BEDSIDE
MANNER (SSE #1492)

Bachelor #4: Dr. Terrance McCall + Dr. Alix Ducane =
Attached at the Hip UNDERCOVER M.D. (SIM #1191)

Bachelor #5: Dr. Peter Sullivan + Raven Songbird = ???
THE M.D.'s SURPRISE FAMILY (SSE #1653)

Chapter One

"Are you God?"

The soft, somewhat high-pitched voice punctured a tiny hole into his train of thought. Seated at his desk and studying a new AMA report regarding brain surgery techniques, Dr. Peter Sullivan looked up sharply. He wasn't expecting anyone. This office was supposed to be his haven, his island away from the noise and traffic just outside his door.

His haven had been invaded.

A boy stood in his doorway. A small-boned, black-haired boy with bright blue eyes. The boy's manner was woven out of not quite a sense of entitlement, but definitely out of a sense of confidence.

He had on an Angels sweatshirt and a pair of jeans that looked baggy on his thin frame.

As the boy looked at him, his perfectly shaped eyebrows wiggled together in a puzzled expression as if, now that he'd asked the question, he had doubts about the assumption he'd made.

Served him right for not making sure his door was properly closed, Peter thought, annoyed at the intrusion. Beyond his door all manner of people wandered the halls of Blair Memorial, especially on the ground floor, where all the doctors's offices were located. But traffic wasn't supposed to leak into here.

He carefully marked his place, then gave his attention to the task of sending the boy on his way.

"Excuse me?" Peter knew his voice could be intimidating. To his surprise, the little boy looked unfazed. Peter didn't feel like being friendly, especially not this morning. He'd heard that one of his patients hadn't made it.

It wasn't supposed to matter.

He purposely distanced himself from the people he operated on, thinking of them as merely recipients of his skills, almost like objects that needed repairing. To approach what he did in any other way was just too difficult for him.

And yet, Amanda Peterson's death weighed heavily on him.

He'd learned of her passing by accident, not by

inquiry, but that didn't change the effect the news had had on him. He'd thought that he'd been properly anesthetized by the knowledge that there was only a two percent chance the woman would survive the surgery, much less the week.

Still, two percent was two percent. A number just large enough to attach the vague strands of hope around.

Damn it, why couldn't he just divorce himself from his emotions? Why couldn't he just not care anymore? Every time he thought he had that aspect of himself under control, something like this would happen and he'd feel that trickle of pain.

Rather than leave, the boy in his doorway crossed into his office, moving on the balls of his feet like a ballet dancer in training.

"Are you God?" he repeated, cocking his head as if that might help him get a clearer handle on the answer.

"No," Peter said with the firm conviction of a neurosurgeon who'd just had God trump him on the operating table. The boy didn't move. "What makes you ask?" Peter finally ventured.

The boy, who couldn't have been more than about seven or eight, and a small seven or eight at that, pulled himself up to his full height and watched him with eyes that were old. "Because Raven told me that you can perform miracles."

"Raven? Is that some imaginary friend?" His

daughter Becky had had an imaginary friend. Seymour. She'd been adamant that he address Seymour by name whenever he'd spoken to the air beside her. There had even been a place for Seymour at the table. And she'd insisted that he say good-night to Seymour every evening after he'd read her a bedtime story, otherwise Becky would look at him with those big brown eyes of hers, waiting.

God, he'd give anything if he could say good-night to Seymour again.

"No," the dark-haired boy told him patiently, "Raven's my sister."

"Well, your sister's wrong." He wondered if he was going to have to escort the boy to the hall. "I'm not God and I don't do miracles."

Because if he could have, if he could have just performed one miracle in his life, it would have been to save Lisa and Becky. He would have willingly and gladly given his own life to save them. But the trade hadn't been his to make.

The small invader seemed unconvinced. "Raven's never wrong."

Peter snorted. Women never thought they were wrong, even short ones. Becky had been as headstrong as they came. He'd always laughed at what he called her "stubborn" face whenever she'd worn it. He couldn't remember the last time he'd laughed.

"First time for everything, kid." He nodded toward the doorway behind the boy. ''Why don't you go now and find her?''

The boy half turned. As if on cue, a woman came up to his doorway. A woman with long, shining blue-black hair and eyes the same intense color blue as the boy's. She was of medium height, slender, with alabaster skin—the kind of woman that would have inspired one of the Grimm Brothers to pick up his pen and begin spinning a story about Snow White. The family resemblance was glaring.

As was the fact that the relieved-looking woman standing in his doorway was very possibly one of the most beautiful women ever created.

Even a man whose soul was dead could notice something like that, Peter thought vaguely.

She could have shaken him, Raven thought, her hands clasping her brother's shoulders. He'd given her a scare. Again. ''Blue, what did I tell you about wandering off?''

''You were talking to that nurse, looking for Dr. Sullivan,'' Blue told her matter-of-factly. He gestured toward the man at the desk. ''I found him for you.''

At seven, Blue had the reading level of a twelve-year-old. He had his father's penchant for absorbing everything and his mother's ability for optimistic interpretation.

Raven pressed her lips together. There was no

arguing with Blue. Talking by the time he was a year old, Blue had been called precocious by her parents. He was their change-of-life miracle baby. Free-spirited, Rowena and Jon Songbird accepted everything that came their way, finding the very best in life and mining that vein until that was all there was.

They'd infused that talent, that view of life, within her ever since she could remember, but there were times when that ability was severely challenged.

Blue's present situation challenged her optimism to the limit.

Raven placed her hand on the boy's shoulder in a protective gesture. "I was asking that nurse directions to the office."

"I know." Blue looked up at her with a smile that took up half his face. "But I found him."

It was more than apparent that he couldn't see what the problem was. Couldn't see why his sister would get upset if he went off on his own as long as he was undertaking the present mission at hand. The offspring of a neo-hippie couple, Blue marched to his own drummer and, at times, the tempo drove her crazy.

For a moment the duo seemed to be completely oblivious to Peter. Not that he minded, but he didn't want it happening while they were taking up space within his office.

"Excuse me," Peter interrupted the exchange. "But just why were you looking for me?"

The woman turned to give him just as radiant a smile as the boy with the improbable name of "Blue" had.

"I'm your ten o'clock appointment." Lacing her arms around the boy she'd drawn closer in front of her, she amended, "We are your ten o'clock appointment."

Peter glanced at his calendar. He didn't have anything scheduled until his one o'clock surgery this afternoon. He raised his eyes to her face. "I'm sorry, but—"

Just then his phone buzzed, interrupting him. Peter yanked up the receiver and said, "Yes?" in less than a friendly tone.

"Oh, thank God you're in." The voice on the other end of the phone breathed a sigh of relief. The voice belonged to Diane, the chief administrator's niece who, as the general secretary, was well-meaning but far less than perfect at her job. "Um, Dr. Sullivan, I think I forgot to let you know that you have a ten o'clock appointment this morning. Did they show up yet?"

"Yes, I'm looking at them right now."

"Oh, good."

"A matter of opinion," he informed her tersely

as he hung up. He didn't like being caught unprepared.

"You weren't expecting us?" Raven concluded.

"Not until this moment." He looked at the boy she was holding in front of her. Children didn't belong in this office. What went on here was far too serious for their childish voices and innocent demeanors. Besides, being around children painfully reminded him that he no longer had one of his own. "Madam, people who come to see me don't usually bring their children—"

The smile she gave him had a very strange, almost tranquilizing effect on him. It seemed to effortlessly enter into every pore of his body like steam.

"He's not my child, he's my brother and, since this concerns him, I thought he should have the opportunity to meet you."

Peter's eyes narrowed. The appointment had been made without his knowledge and he certainly hadn't said whether or not he was going to take the case. "I'm on review?"

She laughed. It was a light, breezy sound that made him think, for no apparent reason, of springtime and tiny green shoots on trees.

She glanced at her brother before answering. "I suppose, in a manner of speaking." The woman indicated the two chairs in front of his desk. "May we?"

For the moment he had no choice but to incline his head. Blue scrambled right up into the chair closest to the desk. Facing him, Blue smiled up at Peter with his sister's mouth, generous and friendly.

The young woman sat down. Rather than perch on the edge, the way he'd seen so many people in this office do, she slid back, making herself comfortable.

Almost succeeding in making him comfortable.

Peter had to pull himself back to recapture the edge he always felt, the edge that separated him from anyone who sat on the other side of the desk. The edge that kept him separate from everyone.

"I've heard you're the best." Raven paused for half a second, in case Dr. Sullivan wanted to pretend to be modest. But when no such pretense materialized, she continued, "But I also wanted to get a feel for you myself."

"A 'feel' for me?"

He stared at her as if she were speaking another language, had descended from another planet. What was she talking about? What went on in this office and the operating room—if he agreed to undertake the surgery—had nothing to do with "feelings." It had to do with facts, with the latest procedures and available technology.

She made him think of some latter day free spirit who had accidentally stepped across a rift in time.

She certainly looked the part with her colorful clothing and her surfboard-straight hair.

"My parents taught me that you could tell a great deal about a person by the way they behaved both on their home territory and on yours." And then she flashed a dazzling smile at him, as if she could read the thoughts running through his mind. "Don't worry, I'm not inviting you to my house."

"Look, Miss—" He stopped, looking to her to fill in the gap.

"Songbird," Raven supplied. "But you might find it easier to call me Raven."

Songbird. It figured. The woman was definitely as flighty as they came. She meandered around enough to imitate the flight pattern of a slightly dizzy bird.

"Miss Songbird, is there a point to this?" he asked impatiently, looking at his watch. He felt as if he was wasting precious time here and as he spoke, Peter began to rise from his chair. "Because if there isn't, then I have got—"

The woman with the mesmerizing, almond-shaped eyes reached out and placed her hand on his, staying his exit. For half a second, immobilized by surprise, Peter left his hand beneath hers. The next moment he pulled his hand back, staring at her as if she were some kind of alien creature. He was willing to concede the point without debate.

"Sorry, still getting a feel for you. You are awfully tense. Are you operating soon?"

Not a retro-hippie, he decided, but a Gypsy. All that was missing was a tambourine and a colorful scarf around her head. She already had the bright outfit. "Just who *are* you?" He wanted to know.

"No," she said as if he'd asked her another question entirely—or was about to, "I don't believe in tarot cards, or fortune-telling, but there is such a thing as an aura and I can feel yours." She felt it prudent not to tell him about her mother's heritage. It might only served to spook him, or worse, to make him more cynical. "It's very, very uptight. Brittle, you might say," she added.

Beyond brittle, he thought. Damn close to broken. His aura, if there was such a thing, had long since been destroyed. Lisa and Becky had been his only reason for living and now they were gone. If he was alive, it was just because he'd been going through the motions for so long, he'd forgotten how to stop.

He looked from the boy to the woman. She'd come in with a manila envelope tucked under her arm. He assumed this visit had something to do with that. "Would you like to tell me why you're here?"

"My brother's pediatrician thought we should come to see you." This time, she did slide forward on the seat, as if what she was saying made her uneasy and she wanted to say it quickly. "Blue has three tumors along his spinal cord. He needs to have them removed as soon as possible,'' she recited as if she'd rehearsed the words for hours in her vanity mirror. ''I have an X ray.'' She laid the large manila envelope on his desk.

With a barely stifled impatient sigh, Peter took out the X ray she'd brought and looked at it. He was aware that the boy was leaning forward and had propped his chin on his fisted hands, staring at the same X ray.

''That's my spinal cord,'' he said as if he knew exactly what a spinal chord was. ''Kind of messed up, isn't it?''

Peter looked at Raven. ''How old did you say he was?''

''I'm seven,'' he said.

''Seven,'' Peter repeated. The same age that Becky had been before... Before. He didn't remember Becky sounding this old. ''He doesn't sound seven.''

''He was reading at three,'' Raven told him proudly.

Peter nodded. ''Impressive.'' He turned his attention to the X ray.

It was the barest of introductions to the problem. He would need extensive films taken if he decided to undertake the surgery. But what he was looking at was enough to tell him that the boy's pediatrician wasn't mistaken. There were indeed tumors clustering at the base of the boy's spinal cord.

"Your brother's pediatrician is right," he informed Raven crisply, sliding the X ray back into the manila envelope.

"Yes, I know." She looked at him. "Dr. DuCane's been Blue's doctor ever since he was a week old and I trust her implicitly. That's why we're here."

He looked from the boy to the woman. "What kind of a name is Blue?"

Blue grinned at Raven and launched into an explanation. "It was the color of the sky my mother was staring at when she gave birth to me in the field."

Peter looked sharply at Blue's sister. Had the boy's mother gone into premature labor while they were out on the road? "'In the field'?"

Raven pressed her lips together, obviously struggling with something. "My mother didn't like hospitals. She said they always made her think about people dying."

He noticed the grim set to the woman's mouth, such contrast to the smile that had been there seconds ago. The change vaguely stirred a question in his mind, but he let it go. He didn't indulge in personal questions, unless they had something to do with the outcome of the surgery. "Is that why she's not here right now?"

"No." Raven took a breath, as if that could somehow buffer the pain that assaulted her each time her mind turned to the subject. "She's not here because she died in a car accident when Blue was two. Both of my parents died in the crash."

She didn't add that they, along with Blue, had been on their way to her college graduation. They'd gotten a late start because her mother had been finishing up a project that was due. In a hurry, they weren't paying strict attention to the road. The highway patrolman told her that a trucker who had fallen asleep at the wheel had plowed right into them.

Blue, in the back seat, had miraculously managed to survive, but both of her parents had died instantly.

She saw an odd expression come over the doctor's face. She was accustomed to looks of pity or sympathy. This was neither. "Is anything wrong, Doctor?"

The words "car accident" had instantly raised myriad thoughts in his head, bringing with it an unwanted image that he strove, every day of his life, to erase from his mind.

He'd been on the scene only minutes after it had taken place.

The surgery had run over and he'd been hurrying home to his family because he'd promised to be there early for once. Lisa and Becky were taking him out for his birthday. He'd had no idea that they had been on their way to the hospital to surprise him. Driving fast, with one eye out for the highway patrol, he'd passed an overturned car on the side of the road.

The scene was already behind him when the delayed recognition had hit him.

He didn't know how many seconds had passed before he'd realized that the mangled blue Toyota hadn't just resembled Lisa's car, it *was* Lisa's car.

He remembered praying as he'd spun his car around. Praying he was wrong. That someone else's family was there, beneath the sheets, and not his.

It was the last prayer he remembered praying. Because the answer had been negative.

Peter blew out a breath slowly, shutting away the memory. Shutting away the pain.

"No," he told her in a dead voice, "nothing's wrong."

Chapter Two

Peter frowned. He could tell the woman sitting in the chair on the other side of the desk was about to launch into a full-fledged recital of her family history. Being trapped here, listening to a long-winded recitation of who had what was the last thing he wanted. It was bad enough that she had brought the boy to the preliminary consultation. He didn't need to see the boy until he'd made up his mind as to what was necessary. After all, it wasn't as if he had X-ray vision to study the boy's problem and, whatever he needed to know, the boy's sister could tell him.

And tell him and tell him.

Peter held his hand up, visually stopping her before she could sufficiently warm up to her subject matter. "I don't need to hear that."

His sharp tone cut her dead.

Raven pressed her lips together. She was beginning to have serious doubts about Dr. DuCane's recommendation. Dr. Peter Sullivan might very well be a wizard with a scalpel in his hand, but for Blue she required more. She required a doctor with something more than ice water in his veins. She wanted a surgeon with a passion for his work and a desire to save every patient he came across. She was beginning to think that Sullivan was not that surgeon.

"Why not?" she asked.

The simple question caught him up short. He wasn't accustomed to being challenged professionally, not by patients or the relatives of patients. There was emotion in her voice, something he strove to keep out of his realm. He never had anything but crisp, clear, economic conversations with the people who entered one of his offices. They told him their problem, usually coming in with extensive scans and films, and he studied the odds of succeeding in the undertaking. He liked beating the odds. It was his way of shaking his fist at the universe.

It was the only time he felt alive.

She was still waiting. The woman honestly expected him to answer. He bit back an exasperated sigh. "Because in this case, it has nothing to do with what is wrong with the patient."

He made it sound so sterile, so detached. Raven looked Dr. Sullivan in the eyes and corrected quietly, but firmly, "Blue." She glanced at her brother. "He has a name."

"And rather an odd one at that." The words had escaped before he'd had a chance to suppress them. Trouble was, he wasn't accustomed to censoring himself—because he rarely spoke at all.

Raven glanced at Blue. To her relief, the doctor's words didn't seem to affect him. She should have realized they wouldn't. Like his parents before him, Blue was a blithe spirit, unaffected by the casual, small hurts that littered everyday lives. It was as if he examined a larger picture than that which everyone else saw. Twenty years her junior, Blue was very precious to her and, she vowed silently, if she had to move heaven and earth, she was going to find a surgeon who could help Blue. Really help.

In her opinion, that surgeon wasn't Dr. Sullivan.

She raised her chin just a tad. Peter noticed for the first time the slightest hint of a cleft in it.

"We prefer to think of it as unusual—just like Blue is." She reached across and took Blue's small hand in hers. She closed her fingers around it. Peter got a sudden image of union and strength. Odd thing to think of when he was looking at a mere slip of a woman. ''Well, Doctor, I think that you've told me all I really need to know.''

Obviously the woman was woefully uninformed. But then, this was his domain, not hers. ''I don't think so. There are CAT scans to arrange to be taken. I need to study those before I agree to do the surgery.''

He had no more emotion in his voice than if he was talking about deciding between which colors to have his office painted. She was right. This wasn't the man for them. Centered, her mind made up, Raven smiled as she shook her head. ''That won't be necessary.''

Peter's eyes narrowed. Feeling like someone whose turf was challenged, he told her, ''I'll decide what's necessary.''

Her eyes never left his. ''No,'' she replied softly but firmly, ''you won't.'' Rising to her feet, she closed her hand a little more tightly around her brother's. ''Thank you for your time, Doctor.''

It took a great deal of conscious effort on his part not to allow his mouth to drop open as she and her brother walked out of his office.

Astonishment ricocheted through him. He had just been rejected. The woman had rejected him. That had never happened to him before. Patients were always seeking him out because he was reputed to be one of the finest neurosurgeons in the country. And ever since he'd found himself without his family, there was nothing left to fill up his hours but his work.

Oh, he stopped by occasionally at Renee's to see how she was doing, but that hardly counted. Renee had been, and in his opinion still was, his mother-in-law. By her very existence, she represented his only connection to Lisa and his past. Besides, he got along with the woman. She was like the mother he could never remember.

Neither he nor Lisa had any siblings. Only children born of only children. It made for a very small Christmas dinner table. Especially since his mother had died when he'd been very young and his father had passed away before he'd ever met Lisa.

He had promised Lisa that they would have a house full of kids. It was a promise he never got to keep.

As twilight crowded in around him, bringing with it a heightened sense of loss, he found himself driving not to the place where he slept night after night, but to the house that had once seemed so cheery to him. The house where he would see Lisa after putting in an inhuman amount of hours at the hospital. Because Lisa had been his bright spot. She had made him laugh no matter how dark his mood.

Now the laughter was gone, as was the brightness. He'd sold his own house shortly after the funeral and moved into a one-bedroom apartment. He didn't require much in the way of living space and the memories within the house they had bought and decorated together had become too much to deal with. He preferred being in a position where he had to seek out the memories rather than have them invade his head every time he looked at anything related to Lisa's or Becky's life.

Peter pulled up in the small driveway and got out. Telling himself that he should be on his way home instead of bothering Renee, he still walked up to her front door. He stood there for a moment before he rang the bell.

Renee had given him a key to the house, but he never used it. He always rang the bell and on those rare times when she wasn't home, he'd turn around and leave. The house where Lisa had grown up was too much to bear without someone there to act as a buffer.

Renee Baker answered the door before the sounds of the bell faded away. A tall, regal-looking woman with soft gray hair and gentle brown eyes, she greeted him warmly as she opened the door.

"I was hoping you'd stop by." She paused to press a kiss on his cheek, then stood back as he crossed her threshold. "You look like hell, Pete." She closed the door behind him. "Bad day?"

He let the warmth within the house permeate him a moment before answering. "There aren't any good ones."

The expression on Renee's face told him that she knew better. "There are if you let them come, Pete." She cocked her head, looking at him. "Did you eat?"

His reply was a half shrug and a mumbled, "Yeah."

Because he wasn't looking directly at her, Renee repositioned herself so that she could peer into his face. "What?"

This time the shrug employed both shoulders. "Something."

She shook her head. The short laugh was a knowing one. "You didn't eat." Turning slowly on her heel, she led the way into her kitchen. "C'mon, I've got leftover pot roast."

He knew better than to argue. So he followed her into the kitchen, because, for a little while, he needed her company. Because he felt as if every day he stood at a critical crossroads and he had no idea which way to go. Today was one of those days when he didn't know why he even continued to place one foot in front of the other.

When his mood was darkest, he came to talk to Renee. And to remember a happier time.

Moving quickly for a woman who wrestled daily with the whimsy of rheumatoid arthritis, never knowing when she would be challenged and when she would receive the green light to move freely,

Renee put out a plate of pot roast and small potatoes. His favorite meal, as she remembered.

Peter said nothing as she prepared the plate.

She gave him a look just before she went to retrieve a bottle of soda from the refrigerator.

"Am I going to have to drag the words out of you?" Then she laughed. "Why should tonight be any different than usual?" she speculated. Placing a glass in front of him, she looked down at Peter. "Talk to an old woman, Pete. Tell me about your day and why you're here tonight instead of last night or tomorrow."

She went to get a glass for herself when she heard him say, "I lost a patient today."

"I'm sorry to hear that." Renee crossed back to the table and helped herself to the bottle of soda. Her voice was filled with understanding. She'd told him more than once that it took a special person to do what he did, day after day, and not break down. "But it does happen. You've saved more than you've lost."

Peter realized that she'd misunderstood him. "No, I don't mean that way. I meant, I lost a patient," he repeated between forkfuls of pot roast that melted on his tongue. "He walked out of my office. Actually, his sister took him away."

Renee set down her glass. "Sister, huh? You probably scared her away."

Not likely, not someone like the woman who'd

been in his office this morning. "I don't scare anyone."

Like a mother studying her child, Renee took his face in her hand and pretended to scrutinize it carefully, just to be certain that she was right. "Not with your looks, Pete, but I have to tell you, you were definitely hiding behind a pillar the day they were teaching all about bedside manners."

He shrugged as she withdrew her hand. "A surgeon doesn't need a bedside manner."

"Don't you believe it. A lot of the times—and especially in the field you're in, Pete—the surgeon is all that stands between the patient and the big sleep. Patients want to hang on to what you tell them. They want you to make them feel better even before they get wheeled into the operating room."

He raised his eyes to hers. He thought she knew him better than that. "I don't deal with giving out false hopes."

Renee sat across from him at the table, nursing the glass of soda she'd just poured for herself. The expression on her face transcended conversation. "The mind is a very powerful tool, Peter. It can perform miracles at times."

He had a great deal of respect for Renee, but her philosophy was completely alien to him. "If people could think themselves well, Renee, there'd be no reason for doctors."

She leaned in closer as she spoke. "That's not

what I meant—exactly. But a patient needs all the help he can get—so does a doctor.'' She looked at him pointedly. ''Use what's available. Make a patient think positive. It can't hurt.'' She smiled encouragingly at him. ''What have you got to lose?''

He could give her the answer without thinking. ''Time.'' And giving a patient empty words was definitely wasting it.

Unfazed, Renee shrugged before she took another sip. ''It goes by anyway. Might as well do something good with it.'' Setting down her glass, she looked at his plate. The four slices she'd put there were gone, as were the tiny potatoes. She nodded at it. ''See, I knew you were hungry.'' She let her eyes travel down his upper torso. ''Come by more often, Pete. You're getting way too skinny.''

He hadn't come here to talk about himself. Reversing the tables on her, he gazed at her for a long moment. Her health was a major concern to him. ''You doing okay?''

Like someone uncomfortable with the subject matter, Renee shrugged dismissively. She'd once told him that the less she thought about the advancing arthritis that sought to conquer her, the better off she was.

''I've got my good days and my bad days, same as everyone else.'' And then she flashed a smile. ''This is a good day.'' Renee glanced at the wheelchair that was tucked away in the corner in the family room. She used it when there was no way around it. But most of the time, she didn't have to resort to it. "That's always there, waiting for me." And then she smiled at him, as if her point was made. "I just think myself out of it."

Peter shook his head. The woman was incorrigible. Just like Lisa had been. Just like Becky had been on her way to becoming. "Whatever works."

Leaning across the table, Renee covered his hand with hers. "That's right. Whatever works. And positive thought works."

He was glad she felt that philosophy worked for her, but it wasn't the way for him. He sincerely doubted that he was capable of thinking positively. Not after the negative event that had traumatized in his life.

The floors smelled of antiseptic and something that had been sprayed to mask the scent. It succeeded only in becoming an annoying hybrid. But the smell would be gone by the time the daily hospital traffic began to weave its way through the halls.

It was early.

He liked the quiet, before the noises started. Normally he would just be heading to the hospital, but he'd arrived at Blair Memorial earlier than usual today. As happened with a fair amount of regularity, sleep had eluded him again last night. He'd spent it tossing and turning, find tiny islands of sleep and snatching them, only to wake up again soon afterward. By four he'd given up the fight.

He decided he might as well get an early start on the day. There was a surgery scheduled for nine this morning and he felt a need to review the CAT scans again. He knew the procedure cold, but he'd always felt that it never hurt to be overprepared.

It beat the hell out of being underprepared.

Preoccupied, he didn't notice her at first. Whenever he was locked into his thoughts, he tended to have tunnel vision to the exclusion of the rest of the world.

But even so, the fact that there was someone sitting in the hallway right outside his office did register in the peripheral portion of his brain, that small space where he allowed life's ordinary little happenings to huddle together.

As he fished out the keys from his pocket, Peter was vaguely aware that the figure rose from the chair. Swirls of color penetrated his consciousness and he glanced in the figure's direction. And was not as surprised as he would have thought he should be.

It was the boy-with-the-funny-name's sister.

She grinned at him broadly. He had the impression of standing beside an overly lit billboard. "Hi."

"Hi," he echoed only because she'd used the

word. Looking around, he saw that she was alone. He'd half thought that if she turned up at all, she would bring reinforcements with her, not fly solo.

He put his key into the lock and turned it. "What are you doing here?"

"Waiting for you," she answered simply, succeeding in mystifying him further.

Not waiting for an invitation as he opened the door, Raven Songbird walked into his office.

He dropped his keys back into his pocket as he looked at her suspiciously. "Why?"

Her face was the picture of innocence. "Because I wanted to talk to you." She'd been waiting for him to show up for almost twenty minutes. Alix DuCane, Blue's pediatrician, had told her that the unfriendly neurosurgeon usually came in early and she'd wanted to catch him before his day got under way.

"There's a handy thing called the telephone." He glanced at the one on his desk for emphasis.

She'd thought about calling him, but had dismissed it. More than likely, she would have gotten his receptionist or the answering service. And she had a feeling that asking him to return the call would have fallen on deaf ears.

Raven told him a little of her philosophy. "I prefer talking to people face-to-face." She could see that didn't sit very well with him. "Are you always so unfriendly, or is it just me?"

"Yes and yes," he answered tartly before asking a question of his own. "Are you always so 'in your face' with people?"

"Mostly."

He wasn't prepared for the smile. Or for the effect it seemed to have on him. Discreetly, he took a breath, as if that would help shield him from this small dynamo who was determined to invade his professional life. "So I haven't been singled out?"

"Well, yes, you have," she allowed, then quickly added, "but not for that. My doctor thinks I should give you a second chance."

"Oh, he does, does he?"

"She," Raven corrected, then supplied the doctor's name. "Dr. Alix DuCane and, actually, she's Blue's doctor, not mine."

He was familiar with the name if not the person. Ducane had been on staff at Blair Memorial for several years and was now head of pediatrics. She'd been here when he'd first arrived. Knowing what he did about the pediatrician, he was surprised that the woman hadn't picked up the phone to call him about this.

"And just why did she recommend this generosity of spirit on your part?"

She'd never liked sarcasm. But this was for Blue, so she was going to put up with it. She would have been willing to put up with the devil himself for

Blue and it was beginning to look as if she just might have to.

"Because Dr. DuCane thinks you really are the best." She'd called the woman after her visit with Dr. Sullivan, not to complain but just to explain why she wasn't about to take the pediatrician's advice. Alix had prevailed upon her to rethink her decision and to give the doctor another chance. Alix had volunteered to provide the bedside manner herself if necessary.

It was time to get to the point. Since he'd begun operating, his patients had all been over the age of eighteen and he now preferred it that way. "I don't do children."

Unlike her late parents and her brother, Raven had a temper she usually kept under wraps. It was the one gene, according to her mother, that her maternal grandfather had contributed to the mix. Jeremiah Blackfeather had never been a mild-mannered man and there were times that Raven felt as if her late grandfather was channeling through her. "From what I see, you don't do people, either, Dr. Sullivan. Just subjects."

The slight show of temper surprised him. For some unknown reason, it also amused him, though he kept that to himself. "And you don't approve."

"I want my brother's life to matter to you."

"A good surgeon doesn't get involved, Ms. Bird."

''Songbird,'' she corrected. Then, for emphasis, she added, ''Like the clothes.''

Peter looked at her, puzzled for a moment, then something clicked into place inside his brain. Lisa had had a wildly colorful blouse she'd absolutely adored. She'd had it on the day she was killed. He'd given it to her on their first anniversary. He remembered the tag because it had been in the shape of a bird. A dove, Lisa had told him.

Peter raised an eyebrow. ''Any connection?''

''My mother started the line.'' She didn't bother hiding her pride. There seemed to be no point to it. ''Dad said they needed to live on more than love and Mom came up with a line of clothing that they sold to their friends. First few years, she worked out of an old VW bus that my dad turned into a workroom for her. Demands kept coming in and—'' She stopped abruptly. She smiled at him. ''You don't want to hear about this.''

''I didn't think I had a choice.'' And then, for just a second, his expression softened as he thought of Lisa wearing the blouse for the first time. ''My wife had a blouse made by your mother. Said it was her favorite thing in the whole world besides Becky—and me.''

''Becky,'' she repeated. Curiosity got the better of her. ''Your daughter?''

''Yes.''

''How old?'' The doctor looked at her strangely.

Wondering what she'd said wrong, Raven clarified, ''Your daughter, how old is she now?''

''She isn't any age now.'' His tone was distant again, hollow. ''My daughter died two years ago in a car accident. Along with her mother.''

That was why he'd looked at her like that yesterday when she'd mentioned the car accident that had claimed her parents. Of all the things they could have had in common, this was really awful, she thought. ''Oh, God, I'm so sorry.''

She'd placed her hand on his shoulder. Not wanting the contact, he moved his shoulder away. ''Yes,'' he said quietly, ''So am I.''

Chapter Three

A little surprised at his reaction, Raven dropped her hand to her side. ''You don't like being touched, do you?''

''Not particularly.''

His tone was so frosty, a person could freeze to death. Raven began having second thoughts again. She wanted the best for Blue, but she was having trouble convincing herself that someone so removed could care more about the patient than he would gaining another cerebral rush.

''You know, I read somewhere that neurosurgeons believe they're above God.''

Peter switched on his computer. The low hum

told him it was going through its paces—just like the ones this woman was putting him through.

"Not above," Peter corrected, "just working in tandem with." He blew out a breath. He didn't have time for this because he was due in surgery in an hour. "Look, I don't think you came back here to check out my divinity, or lack thereof. Do you want me to consider taking your brother on as a patient or not?"

"No, I don't want you to consider taking him on." She saw the surgeon raise his eyebrows in surprise, so she drove home her point. "I want you to take him. Blue has an incredible zest for life. I'd like for him to be able to run through it, not restricted in any way."

He was a realist, weighing the downside rather than the up. Whatever optimism he'd once possessed, the car accident had taken away from him. "That might not be possible."

Raven refused to allow any negative thoughts to enter into this. She had to believe the surgery was going to be a success. Anything else was unthinkable.

"It *will* be possible, Dr. Sullivan, if you come on board."

Just yesterday, he thought, she'd been skeptical, doubting not his ability but his heart. He wondered if he should tell her that he didn't have one. "Despite my emotional distance?"

"After due consideration, I don't think that'll be a problem. You see, Blue likes you." They'd talked about it last night and the boy seemed perfectly willing to put his fate in Sullivan's hands. She placed a lot of stock in rapport. "If Blue likes you, you can't help but like him back." That, to her, was a given. She'd never met anyone who hadn't warmed to the boy, usually instantly. "It's a gift he got from my mother."

"Whether I like him or not has nothing to do with the surgery."

There was a knowing look in her eyes he found annoying. As if she was privy to some secret he wasn't allow to know. "I disagree."

Peter frowned as he typed in his password. She'd almost made him forget it. When was the last time that had happened? He was nothing if not organized.

"You're free to disagree until the cows come home, that doesn't alter the outcome."

She laughed, a wave of nostalgia undulating over her. "Until the cows come home? I haven't heard that expression since I was a little girl—and they really did come home." She saw his eyebrows knit themselves together in a quizzical wavy line despite plainly visible efforts to resist curiosity. Maybe the man was a little more human than he liked to think. "We lived on a farm. My parents wanted the simple life."

"Songbird, Inc. is a Fortune 500 company."

"They *wanted* the simple life," Raven repeated, emphasizing the crucial word, "but it kind of got complicated along the way." Her parents had been wonderful people, taken much too soon. She wanted the whole world to know just how noble, how good they really were. Even this cynical man. "Not so they lost any of their initial values. They just had a lot bigger house to place those values in toward the end. My mother actually did sew every prototype, every new garment she created."

He paused, trying to imagine the life the woman in his office must have led. It was probably something of a merger between latter day hippies and the captains of industry.

"What did your father add to this mix?"

"He played guitar while she sewed." If she closed her eyes, she could almost see him. Sitting by the white stone fireplace, playing one of the songs he'd written while her mother worked on a loom, creating the fabric that would eventually find itself fashioned into a dress or a blouse or a scarf.

Nobody lived like that, he thought. Raven Songbird probably gleaned the scenario from some afternoon movie written for TV. One in which the woman worked while the man sat noodling around on some instrument or other. "Very productive."

There was that cynical tone again. Hadn't this

man ever had a good day in his life? "Actually, it inspired her."

Peter heard the defensive note in Raven's voice. He realized it probably sounded as if he was criticizing her family. She had enough to deal with. "That wasn't meant to be critical."

"Yes it was," she contradicted, then followed with an absolving smile. "But you can't help that. You're from a whole different world." Considering what he did for a living, he probably had no idea what "mellowing out" meant. "There's a great deal of pressure involved in working toward becoming a doctor."

"There's a great deal of pressure once you become one, too." Peter stopped abruptly. He had no idea why he'd added that or why he'd shared a single feeling with this diminutive woman who somehow still managed to come across as slightly larger than life.

Needing a diversion, if only for a second, he punched in several letters on the keyboard. His schedule for the next two months appeared on the screen. He scanned it. It was more than full. Work, although not his salvation, kept him from dwelling on his loss and the way his days and evenings felt so hollow. And the times when a fourteen-hour day wasn't enough to fill that hole, several times a year he volunteered his services to Doctors Without Borders, a nonprofit organization that provided free medical care to the poor of the world.

As it stood right now, there was hardly enough room on his schedule to fit in a breath, much less another challenging surgery. He glanced up from the monitor. By all rights, he should turn Raven Songbird away. Give her and her vivacious personality a referral.

But as he began to frame the words, he made the mistake of looking at her. Specifically, at her eyes. There was something eloquent and tender within the blue orbs, not just the humor with which she peppered her words, but something more. Something that made him feel that if he turned her and her brother away, he would be guilty of an unspeakable crime.

Peter was far more surprised than she was to hear himself say, "Why don't you bring Blue back tomorrow morning and we'll see about getting back on the right footing."

He watched, mesmerized as the smile on her face blossomed until he felt as if it spread to him, as well.

"What time?"

He had consultations lined up back to back both at the hospital and in his private office across the street from Blair. The two open three-hour blocks had surgeries packed into them. There wasn't even time for lunch. It wouldn't be the first time he'd eaten in snatches, between patients. "How does seven in the morning sound?"

"Early."

He sighed, thinking, looking for an alternative. His last surgery was at five. If all went well, it would end at eight. "There's nothing open until—"

She didn't let him finish. Her bright smile cut through his words before he could get them all out. "Early's good," she assured him. "I'm usually up at five. Blue doesn't sleep in much later than that."

"Five?"

"Five."

"Voluntarily?" He tried not to stare at her mouth. The smile made it difficult not to.

She nodded. "It's a holdover from living on the farm. You had to be up early to take care of chores before school started."

He shook his head and laughed, realizing that for the first time in weeks, he was actually amused by something. "This is beginning to sound like pages from *Little House on the Prairie.*"

Raven's laugh echoed in the wake of his. He found himself liking the sound a little more each time he heard it. He usually wasn't aware of laughter, because he usually wasn't aware of any kind of happiness, other than when he told members of a family that the patient would pull through. Ordinarily, he left that sort of thing up to whoever was assisting him. The less personal contact he had with people, the better. It was just too much of an effort otherwise.

But this bird-woman left him no choice. He didn't like not having a choice.

"At times," she was saying to him, "it felt a little like that, too."

He found himself staring at her, at her mouth when she laughed, at her eyes when she looked at him. With effort, he reined himself in and focused on what they both needed him to be: Blue's surgeon, nothing else.

And as such, there were procedures he needed to outline for her, things that had to be done before a prognosis.

"Before I see your brother tomorrow, I'm going to need those scans I mentioned yesterday." Opening a drawer, Peter frowned. He didn't find what he expected. Annoyed, and doing a bad job of disguising it, he played hide-and-seek with two more drawers before locating the hospital order forms in a fourth. He pulled one off the top and began writing instructions across the bottom. He signed his name with a flourish, then slowly printed the boy's name in the space at the top.

"Take this to Imaging on the first floor," he told her as he wrote.

"Don't I need an appointment?"

"You'll have one by the time you get there," he assured her. "Ten o'clock, all right?"

She was surprised that Sullivan was actually asking rather than ordering. Blue was in school right now, but she could easily get him out. That gave her more than an hour to get back.

"Ten'll be terrific."

"All right." Finished, he put down his pen. "Just present this when you get there." He held out the form to her.

Taking it, Raven squeezed his hand. "Thank you, Doctor. You're not going to regret this."

He already was, he thought, as he watched her leave the office.

The boy looked smaller to him this time.

Sitting in the chair that he had occupied a little more than a day ago, Blue Songbird seemed to have mysteriously gotten smaller. Or the chair had somehow gotten larger.

Or maybe it was the gravity of what he had seen on the scan that was affecting the way he viewed the boy, Peter thought, making him seem so vulnerable.

Calling the Imaging department as soon as the boy's sister had left his office yesterday, he'd told the woman on the other end of the line to put a rush on the procedure. Because of his standing in the medical community, not to mention Blair Memorial itself, the receptionist knew better than to offer even a single word of protest or to point to the fact that they were already overbooked, overworked and understaffed for the amount of scans and films they had to take and review.

Instead she'd offered a pleasant, "Yes, Doctor," and promised to do her best. He'd ended the conversation by telling her he certainly hoped so.

As he'd hung up, he could almost hear the woman cowering. A tinge of guilt pricked him before he'd blocked it. He was not in the business of making friends, he was in the business of extending lives, of making them more tolerable for people who, through no fault of their own, were faced with intolerable alternatives. Everyone had a purpose in life, and healing was his.

As he looked over his shoulder at the backlit display on the wall and the CAT scan held in place with metal clips, he remembered why he didn't, as a general rule, operate on children. Because as impervious as he tried to make his heart to the life-and-death situations he dealt with, the plight of someone so young faced with something so devastating got to him.

As if reading his mind, the small boy in the large chair smiled brightly at him. It seemed as if he was somehow trying to convey the thought that the situation was not as dire as it appeared. That everything would be all right if he just had a little faith.

It was entirely unfounded optimism. Peter knew that he lived in a world where everything that could go wrong did go wrong. And, more likely than not, with heavy consequences.

Peter suppressed a sigh he felt to the very bottom of the soles of his feet. A kid of seven wasn't supposed to be faced with things like this. He was supposed to be able to run, to laugh and to feel immortal.

Like Becky.

Peter banked down the thought before it could go any further. He shifted his eyes toward Raven. She was unusually quiet for a woman who had verbally accosted him not once but twice. What they had to talk about was not meant for a child's ears. "Are you sure you want him here?"

Blue answered before his sister had a chance to. He answered with the voice and attitude of a young adult who had always been allowed to think freely, who felt that his thoughts mattered as much, not more, not less, than the next person's. That person usually being Raven. "It's my body."

Strange, strange family, Peter thought with a resigned shrug. He looked at Raven again.

"As we've already determined, Dr. DuCane was right. There are tumors on your brother's spinal column. Initially it looked like a cluster, but in actually there seem to be four. Four small tumors."

"That doesn't sound like so many," Blue offered.

One was too many if it was the wrong kind or in

the wrong place. And, in this case, it might be both. Tests would have to be done on the actual tissues before they could discover if the tumors were malignant or not. In his experience, Peter thought grimly, given their location, they usually turned out to be the former. If nothing was done and the tumors were left where they were, it was only a matter of time before they would grow larger and eventually paralyze this boy who had life pulsing from every pore.

Well, there you had it. He did have tumors, Raven thought. Her fingers and toes felt numb. All this time, she'd been secretly holding her breath, praying that there'd been some mistake, that the initial X ray that Dr. DuCane had authorized was erroneous, that the pains in his back were nothing more than just good, old-fashioned growing pains.

But deep down she'd known it wasn't a mistake. That there was something very, very wrong with this perfect little boy.

Raven felt the sting of tears and instantly forced them away. She wasn't about to cry in front of Blue. If she was anything other than upbeat, he would sense it and it would make him worry. Worse, it would make him afraid. There was no way she was going to allow that to happen. He had to feel that this was just something he had to go through and that, at the end, he would be perfect again.

Just as he'd always been.

Peter glanced toward the boy's sister. For a second he thought he saw the shimmer of tears in her eyes. But in the next moment that smile of hers was fixed in place and she was nothing short of confidence personified.

He only wished he felt half that confident.

Raven took a deep breath. "So, Dr. Sullivan, when can you operate?"

"You understand that the operation is extremely delicate?" he said.

If successful, the boy would heal faster than an adult, but there would still probably be therapy, still a painful recovery period to face. And that was *if* everything went right. There were no guarantees. A great deal could go wrong that was beyond anyone's control. He knew that better than anyone.

Raven nodded. She placed her hand over Blue's and gave it a squeeze along with an encouraging smile. She kept her voice cheerful. "That's why we came to you."

"Yeah."

Peter turned his chair around, looking at the CAT scan. Thinking. As with a great many neurological problems, time was of the essence, but they did have a little leeway. He wanted Raven to use that leeway to carefully think things over before she gave him the okay to go ahead.

This wasn't the kind of dilemma a boy of seven should be privy to, even if it was his body. Turning his chair back around, he looked at Blue. ''I'd like to talk to your sister alone.''

Rather than being upset, Blue looked resigned. ''Whatever you tell Raven, she's only going to tell me later.''

''That's up to her.'' And undoubtedly, the woman could couch this a great deal better than anything he could say to the boy. He'd lost the knack of talking to children, not that he'd really ever had it. It was just that Becky had talked to his heart and that was how he communicated with her.

''Okay.'' Blue rose and crossed to the doorway.

''Wait for me in the hall,'' Raven told him. After Blue let himself out and closed the door behind him, she looked at the surgeon expectantly. She supposed it was better this way, after all. Dr. Sullivan might say something to make Blue feel that the surgery wouldn't go well. ''All right, we're alone. What is it you want to tell me?''

Without the boy to listen, Peter felt less restrained. ''Are you aware of the risks involved?''

''I think I am. I've been reading everything I can get my hands on ever since Dr. DuCane told me what she suspected.''

He didn't bother mincing words. ''If I operate, he might still become paralyzed.''

''If you don't, he definitely will.''

Like the rest of his body structure, the boy's spinal cord would be small, delicate. Peter had the hands of a skilled surgeon, but he didn't like taking chances if he could help it. ''There's a small chance—''

She knew what he was about to say. Raven shook her head. ''Too small to take. I believe in meeting problems head-on instead of hiding from them.''

''There's also the fact that the tumors might be malignant—''

Her eyes met his. She could feel the air backing up in her lungs again. ''Yes?''

''If that's the case, the operation might cause the malignancy to spread—''

''Let sleeping dogs lie, is that it?'' She smiled, shaking her head. She wasn't about to place her head in thc sand and hopc for thc bcst. Shc had to tackle this and *then* hope for the best. ''It might spread anyway—*if* it's malignant and there's no proof that it is,'' she informed him with feeling.

He'd found that when emotions were involved, the right decision was not always made. It was best to make decisions after the heat had left and things had cooled off. ''Ms. Songbird, I want you to think about this—''

''My name is Raven,'' she told him, ''And I *have* thought about it.''

He sincerely doubted it. He heard the passion in her voice, the urgency. He didn't want her making a final decision like that. ''Think about it some more,'' he countered. ''We have a small window of time. Use it.''

She blew out a breath, trying not to sound as impatient as she felt. God, why weren't her parents here? She needed someone to lean on. ''How long am I supposed to look through this window?''

Now she was being rational. ''At least twelve hours, twenty-four would be better.''

Raven nodded her head. ''All right,'' she told him even though she already knew what the decision was going to be.

Chapter Four

"What did I ever do to deserve you?" Renee smiled warmly at her son-in-law. Then, grasping the wheels of the wheelchair she'd been forced to use today, Renee scooted herself back from the front door.

"You had Lisa."

Peter entered, his arms full of the groceries he'd stopped to pick up. He'd called her earlier to see if he'd left his jacket at her house the other night. It had been an excuse to talk to the one person who made him feel comfortable, the one person he didn't feel he had to keep his guard up around. The tired note in Renee's voice had alerted him. He knew that this was one of her bad days.

Being Peter, he'd asked about it. She'd been slow to confirm his suspicions. Further pushing on his part had informed him that she hadn't been able to get out of the house to go to the store. He'd volunteered to go for her, picking up the few things she'd admitted that she needed.

Peter made his way to the kitchen and placed the three grocery bags on the counter. Without waiting for Renee to say anything, he began to unpack them. He knew his way around her kitchen as well as she did.

"Have you taken the anti-inflammatory medication I prescribed for you?" he asked casually.

Renee came to a stop directly behind him. She'd gotten far better at managing her wheelchair around corners than she was happy about. But she'd resigned herself to the necessary evil.

"No."

He looked at his mother-in-law over his shoulder, noting that she avoided eye contact. "Have you even bothered to have it filled?"

"I will, I will," Renee assured him, and then she sighed. "It's just that I don't like being foggy."

He gave her a look. They both knew she was just being stubborn. "It won't make you foggy."

Renee waved her hand dismissively. "They *all* make me foggy, or nauseous or something." With another resigned sigh, she said to him what she always said at times like this. "It'll pass, it always does.'' And then she smiled. ''But thanks for worrying.''

He mumbled something unintelligible as he got back to unpacking and storing. ''You know that patient I told you I lost?''

Immediate interest entered her eyes. He knew she liked something to chew on. ''The one who walked out with her brother because of your less than warm-and-toasty bedside manner?'' He nodded in response. ''Did she have a change of heart?''

Heart, that was the word that best suited Raven Songbird, he thought. She displayed a great deal of it in every word she uttered. ''She showed up at the hospital yesterday, said she'd changed her mind.''

Placing the carton of milk on her lap, Renee propelled herself to the refrigerator to put the item away. ''Guess she knows quality when she sees it, even if you have to make a cactus seem warm and cuddly sometimes.''

It felt as if he fought a two-front war. ''It's not my job to coddle them,'' he reminded her.

The look Renee gave him showed she was completely unconvinced. ''Well, there we disagree. Sometimes that *is* part of the job.''

Peter paused, shaking his head. ''That's what she said.''

Approval shone in her hazel eyes. ''Smart cookie. What's her name?''

Peter had to think for a second. He'd never been

very good with names. ''Raven,'' he finally said. ''Raven Songbird.''

The second half gallon of milk on her lap, Renee paused in midroll to look at him with something akin to surprise and awe. ''Like the clothes?''

He nodded. ''Exactly like the clothes.'' He figured Renee might get a kick out of it. After all, the woman could have been a contemporary of hers. ''Her mother started the company.''

Slipping the milk onto the shelf, Renee closed the refrigerator door again. ''Well, I guess she can afford the best—and you are.''

It was no secret that he didn't come cheap. His fee was right at the top of his field, but then, the amounts that he charged enabled him to do his volunteer work for Doctors Without Borders. The fees he collected from his wealthier clients help to fund the operations that he performed on the devastated citizens of Third World countries. In so doing, he wound up bringing hope to the hopeless. Given that he felt no hope himself, he was struck by the irony of the situation.

Peter paused to kiss the top of his mother-in-law's silver head. ''Flattery will get you everywhere,'' he told her with a smile.

''Oh, good.'' She said the words with such feeling, he stopped folding the paper bags and looked at her. ''Because I have something to tell you.''

Putting the empty bags on the side of the table,

he pulled a chair to him, straddled it and looked at her across the table. ''Okay, what?''

Renee took a deep breath. It wasn't a subject she was looking forward to, only one that she knew needed broaching. Until now, she'd allowed him to have his bleeding heart. But she knew her daughter wouldn't have wanted him to continue grieving this way, not for this long. There was no easy way to begin. ''It's been more than two years since Lisa and Becky were taken.''

Peter could feel himself tensing as he looked at her warily. ''Yes?''

Renee reached across the table and touched his hand. ''And I think it's time you moved on.''

''Moved on? Moved on how?'' He knew exactly how she meant, but he wasn't about to give in to that. ''I'm working.''

Renee left her hand where it was, feeling that her son-in-law needed the human contact. ''Yes, I know, but I think that you should do more than work.''

Peter shrugged as he glanced away. ''There's not enough time—''

She watched him pointedly, remembering another Peter. A happier Peter. She missed him. And she had a feeling that Peter missed him, as well. ''There was when you were married.''

''There was a reason to have time when I was married,'' he informed her flatly.

Because he understood what Renee was attempting to do, he forced a smile to his lips. The woman's heart was in the right place, if a little off kilter. ''I have my work and I have you, Renee.'' He brought her hand to his lips and kissed it in the courtly fashion he knew she loved. ''That's enough for me.''

Renee was not about to be dissuaded. ''It shouldn't be. Not that I'm undermining what you do,'' she was quick to explain. ''Your work is very, very important. You perform miracles. But *I* am a poor substitute for what you really need.'' And she knew that he couldn't fight her on that score.

He truly loved Lisa's mother. She was the mother he had never known as a boy, so he humored her where he wouldn't anyone else. ''And what is it that I need?''

Renee set her mouth firmly. ''Female companionship.''

He gestured toward her. ''In case you missed it, you're a female, Renee.''

She snorted at the weak attempt to deflect her focus. ''I'm old enough to be your mother.''

His smile was broad as he took her hand in his. ''I like older women.''

Renee pulled her hand away, giving him a stern, motherly look. ''Peter—''

''Don't,'' he warned her quietly. He saw compassion enter her eyes. ''Maybe someday I'll be ready.'' Although he sincerely doubted it. ''But right now, this is all I can manage.'' In a rare, unguarded moment of honesty, he admitted to her what he barely admitted to himself. ''I'm lucky to be sane.'' And then he shrugged off the moment. ''I didn't exactly have a thriving social life before Lisa, so this is business as usual for me.'' Peter took his mother-in-law's hand in his. ''I know you mean well, Renee, but this is something that'll work itself out.''

Renee closed her hand over both of his. ''Don't hide from life, Pete,'' she told him. ''You have far too much to offer—and so does life,'' she added pointedly. Then, she withdrew her hands and looked at him through the eyes of a mother. ''Now then, have you eaten?''

He laughed, shaking his head. ''I didn't come here for you to feed me, Renee.''

''Well, you're not leaving until I see you have something.'' She pulled away from the table, pivoting the wheelchair so that she could access the refrigerator. ''It's the least I can do.''

Peter rose to his feet. He hated seeing her relegated to that chair. ''No,'' he contradicted, ''the least you can do is let me get that prescription filled for you.''

She turned from the refrigerator and sighed, surrendering. ''I guess one of us has to stop being stubborn first.''

He grinned back. ''Guess so.''

With a resigned nod of her head, Renee propelled herself over to the drawer beside the sink where she kept all the miscellaneous things that she had no given place for. Opening it, she riffled through myriad papers and odds and ends until she found the prescription he had written for her. It was dated several weeks ago and was for a brand-new anti-inflammatory drug that had hit the market.

She held the paper out to him. He knew which pharmacy she frequented. "Go—" she waved Peter on his way "—fill it."

Triumphant, he gave her a knowing smile. "Thought you'd never ask."

"By the way," she called after him. On his way to the front door, he turned to look at her. "Before I forget, next time you see the Songbird girl, see if you can get a scarf for me." Her face softened and she looked like a young girl, he thought, not an older woman imprisoned in a wheelchair. "I always loved their colors."

"I'll see what I can do," he promised before heading out.

The phone was ringing by the time he walked into his apartment later that evening. An emergency? he wondered. Undoubtedly it was his answering service. He'd just left the only person who would have called him privately. After Lisa and Becky had died, people didn't know what to say to him and he had no idea how to field their pity. Eventually, all the friends he and Lisa had had together drifted out of his life.

Pushing the door closed behind him, he quickly crossed to the kitchen where the phone hung on the wall and picked up the receiver.

''Sullivan.''

''You don't keep banker's hours, do you?''

He knew it was *her*. Even though he'd never spoken to Raven on the telephone before, he could tell it was her. The sound of her voice over the line was a little deeper than it was in person, a little like brandy at room temperature, swishing along the sides of a glass. But it was unmistakable.

Now what? he wondered. And how had she gotten his number? While his office numbers were a matter of record, his home line was not listed. ''Ms. Songbird?''

''Raven,'' she reminded him. ''We agreed that you were going to call me Raven.''

''You agreed,'' he pointed out stiffly. ''I said nothing.''

The momentary pause on the other end told him that she'd decided not to argue the point. Instead she got to what he imagined was the crux of her phone call. ''You told me to think about it.''

''I told you to take your time.''

''Time is relative,'' Raven informed him, her

tone blithe. ''I've used enough of it. I'd like to come talk to you.''

He tried to figure out where to fit her in. For that matter, he was going have to do some heavy juggling to fit the boy's surgery into his schedule. ''You could come by the office tomorrow, or the hospital—'' As he spoke, he reached into his pocket for his P.D.A. He needed a clearer idea of what tomorrow looked like before telling her a time.

''Are you free right now?'' When he made no immediate response, she added, ''because if you are, I'd like to meet somewhere now.'' Her voice picked up a little momentum as she spoke. The image of a locomotive, leaving the station, flashed across his mind. ''I want to talk to you as a person, not a doctor.''

Her request was highly irregular, but then, in the very short time that he'd known her, he had gotten the impression that Raven Songbird was by definition highly irregular.

His first instinct was to refuse her request. He wasn't going to be operating on her brother as a person, but as a doctor, a surgeon, and it was in that capacity that he could advise her. He had the feeling that she required something different, something more of him, and even without naming it, he knew he wouldn't be able to accommodate her.

So it was with complete surprise that he heard himself saying, ''Where?''

There was relief and pleasure in her voice when she answered. ''A restaurant or a sidewalk, doesn't matter. You name the place.''

The woman was nothing if not highly unorthodox. ''A sidewalk?''

''Yes.'' She made it sound as if it was the most natural suggestion in the world. ''We could go for a walk.'' There was the tiniest hesitation before she added. ''I just don't want you thinking that I was fishing for a free meal.''

''Never crossed my mind.'' And it hadn't. From the limited information he had about Songbird, Inc., her company could buy any one of a number of restaurants out of petty cash.

''Restaurant,'' he said, not wanting to be put in the position of endless wandering around with a woman who could quite probably talk for all eternity.

''Okay.'' She'd called prepared. ''Are you acquainted with the Hawaiian Inn? It's a little restaurant on Pacific Coast Highway down in Laguna—''

How, with all the places in the area to chose from, had she landed on that particular one? ''I'm acquainted with the restaurant,'' he responded stonily.

''Is it all right with you?'' she pressed. ''Because if it's not—''

He didn't want her speculating about why the restaurant wasn't acceptable to him. The simplest thing was just to agree to it. ''It's all right with me,'' he told her.

''Perfect. I'll see you there, say, in about half an hour.''

''Sounds fine,'' he responded before hanging up.

But it wasn't.

As he drove to the Hawaiian Inn, Peter tried not to remember the last time that he had been there. Tried not to recall the sound of happy voices inside the car as he'd driven to the restaurant.

With his already busy schedule, he'd had to do some fancy rearranging, but it had been worth it. Worth carving out a rare evening on the town with the wife he adored. It had been a celebration of sorts. He and Lisa had just decided to try for a second child. Driving that misting evening, he had been feeling very good about life in general.

The following week, life had irrevocably changed, taking with it any reason to ever feel good about life again.

Strange that the woman should have picked this place, he thought as he pulled up in the lot. Getting out of his car, he hurried up to the front entrance. He'd almost told her no, but then Renee's voice had echoed in his head, telling him that he needed to move on.

He couldn't argue that. He needed to face life if only because he was all that remained of his union.

Continuing was a tribute to the woman he'd loved, to the family he'd lost. Their memory remained alive as long as he did.

Peter walked up to the dark mahogany double doors. Faces of Hawaiian gods, long lost in myth, were carved into the wood. He pulled one of the doors open and walked in. Warmth and noise greeted him.

For a moment he stood just inside the entrance. Remembering. It was as if nothing had changed, certainly not the restaurant. It was just as busy, just as cluttered as he'd recalled. The owners had gone through a great deal of trouble to make the interior look like a thatched hut. As he recalled, the prices on the menu gave testimony that simplicity did not come cheap.

To his right was a five foot reproduction of a Tiki. He looked around it, wondering if he should have waited for Raven outside. Now that he thought of it, she hadn't mentioned where she was going to meet him.

Someone tapped him on the shoulder. Turning, he found that she had solved his dilemma. Raven Songbird, wearing something comprised of swirling blues, greens and yellows, stood right behind him.

Her smile was every bit as warm as the restaurant seemed to be. ''You made it.''

''Apparently.'' He knew his reply sounded curt, but he began to think that maybe he'd made a mistake, agreeing to meet her here. He wasn't the master of emotions even though he liked to think that he was. ''Did you just get here?''

''No, I've been here for a little bit.'' She pointed to a tiny table for one located on the side. There was a bar just beyond it. ''Long enough to order one of those fruity drinks they're so famous for. We can just sit here,'' she suggested, nodding at the table. ''Or we could walk along the beach.''

Something else he'd done with Lisa. Peter shook his head. He didn't feel right about walking along the sand in the moonlight with someone else.

''Here's fine,'' he told her. He glanced around for a waitress. Spying one, he waved the young woman over. The hibiscus tucked behind her ear seemed to be too large for her.

''Yes, sir, what can I get you?''

''A beer. Whatever's handy,'' he added when she began to ask what kind. He had no preference as long as it was cold.

Raven took a seat. Her mouth quirked in amusement as she picked up her pink and foamy drink. ''Beer, huh?'' She used the tip of her umbrella to carefully spear the cherry that was bobbing up and down. ''I didn't take you for a beer drinker.''

He made himself as comfortable as he could opposite her, still wondering what he was doing here. ''Why not?''

She lifted a shoulder in a half shrug. The colorful

material slipped off, she tugged it back over her shoulder. "I envisioned you tipping back something fancy."

A cynical expression drifted across his features before disappearing again. "My father was a dock worker in Baltimore. Formal meant changing his T-shirt more than once a week."

He didn't sound as if he liked the man very much, Raven thought. She couldn't imagine not loving your father. "Where is he now?"

"He died while I was still in medical school." Realizing that he'd given out more personal information than he'd intended, he looked at her sharply. "Did you ask to see me to quiz me about my family?"

Finishing the cherry, she placed the umbrella on the cocktail napkin. "No, I asked you here to get a feeling for Peter Sullivan, the man."

He frowned at her. "You want Peter Sullivan the surgeon operating on your brother, not the man."

"Yes, I know, but the two are a package deal." She saw impatience crease his brow. This was a great deal harder than she'd anticipated. Ordinarily, people talked to her freely. She was usually able to put them at ease. "You can bill me for a consultation." She saw him open his mouth, but beat him to the punch. "As a matter of fact, I insist on it. That way, you won't feel as if I'm trying to take advantage of the situation."

He didn't want her thinking that she had the upper hand here. She didn't. He was in control at all times. He *needed* to be. Because allowing control to slip through your fingers meant being at the mercy of fate—and he knew what fate did to you. It kicked you in the teeth just when you thought happiness was yours.

"You can only take advantage if I let you," he told her pointedly.

She read between the lines. "Tough as nails?" There was a smile on her face, and then it faded just a little. "What do you care about, Peter?"

He didn't like the fact that she felt free enough to strip away the formal layers between them. "That doesn't matter."

She moved her head slowly from side to side. "Oh, but it does to me." Leaning over the tiny table, she tried to make him understand. "I need you to tell me you care about something, Peter. White mice, sunsets, endangered species—it doesn't matter what, just something." She desperately needed to know that the man who would be operating on her brother was someone who cared about the outcome.

He knew he should just get up and leave. But there was something in her eyes… Something that kept him in his seat. Something that had him answering her invasive question. "I care about my mother-in-law."

A smile curved her mouth. ‘‘Wow, there’s a first.’’ He found himself watching, mesmerized as her smile continued to bloom. ‘‘Tell me about her.’’

‘‘She’s a little like you. Pushy.’’ He thought of what Renee had called out to him as he’d left for her prescription. ‘‘She wanted me to ask you for a scarf.’’

‘‘Done.’’ To his surprise, she opened her purse and produced a folded scrap of colorful material, which she handed to him. ‘‘I want you to do my brother’s surgery.’’

He took the scarf and put it into his jacket pocket. ‘‘Because I care about my mother-in-law?’’

‘‘Yes.’’

‘‘You’re a very odd young woman.’’

She laughed softly as she raised the drink to her lips. ‘‘You’re not the first to say that.’’

Chapter Five

The wind was getting serious again, growing chilly, reminding everyone that winter, even in Southern California, was definitely here. As he and Raven stepped outside the restaurant, Peter thought to himself that he should have remembered to wear his coat.

But things like coats and weather were huddled together in the second or third tier of his thoughts, never foremost in his mind. Now that he was no longer a family man, that area was strictly reserved for the surgical procedures that were second nature to him.

Peter turned up his collar and looked out into the

vast parking lot, trying to remember where it was that he had left his vehicle. Though preoccupied, he soon realized that the woman beside him was touching his arm. Trying to invade his space even more than she already had. He raised his brow in a silent query.

"I'd like you to come home with me to tell Blue yourself that you're going to be doing his surgery," she said.

"Ms. Songbird—"

Her eyes touched his. He could almost physically feel her gaze. "Raven," she reminded him.

"Raven—"

And then he stopped. She had a look on her face that he couldn't begin to describe. It occurred to him that sailors, drawn by the siren's song, saw an expression akin to this on the face of an angel just before their ships splintered all around them.

"What?" Peter took a breath, bracing himself.

Her eyes crinkled just a little as she continued watching at him. "Nothing, I just like the way you say my name."

"You mean, under duress?"

The laughter was soft, making him think of gentle breezes and hope springing eternal. He had to be getting punchy.

"I'm not forcing you, I'm asking you," she told him softly.

Not only her expression, but her voice began to

seep into him, like early morning mist that seemed so innocuous, but somehow managed to drench you if you walked in it long enough.

She drenched him.

"Raven," he repeated more firmly, trying to distance himself from this woman and having a harder and harder time doing it. She was like quicksand, he suddenly realized. The more he pulled against her, the more he felt himself being held fast and going under.

This was ridiculous.

This was also what came of putting in eighteen- to twenty-hour days. If he didn't watch himself, his patients were going to suffer. And that was absolutely unacceptable. He might not want to regard them as anything more than items in need of repair, but neither did he want to view them as recipients of possible failed surgeries. Each and every one of them had been brought to him to be made whole again and there was no way he was about to shirk that shoulder-crushing responsibility.

He attempted one last time to detach himself. "Raven, I think the news would come better from you. You handle the P.R., I'll handle the surgery," he added glibly.

"He likes you," she reminded him.

"Your brother doesn't even *know* me," Peter declared, taking no trouble to hide his annoyance.

But if she was the target of that anger, she allowed it to bounce right off her. "He's met you twice now. It doesn't take much for Blue to form opinions." Here came that smile again, the one that could disarm him faster than a high-powered magnet could yank a gun out of an assailant's hand. "And he's usually right."

He sighed, shaking his head. A couple maneuvered past them on their way to the front entrance. Stepping aside, he found himself standing closer to Raven than he'd intended. "So, what, now you're going to tell me that your brother is some kind of psychic?"

"No, just that he's rather intuitive when it comes to people."

He nodded, remembering she'd mentioned something like that to him the other day. "So you said."

She smiled at him, smoke penetrating through the minuscule, almost unperceivable cracks of a thick brick wall. "You were paying attention."

"I *always* pay attention. There're just times when I don't chose to acknowledge the fact," he said.

Her eyes looked as if she was retaining some secret amusement. "I'll keep that in mind."

Why should she bother? he wondered. After the surgery and the two standard follow-up visits, the chances were very high that he and Raven would never interact again. From somewhere deep within the recesses of his mind and soul, the single word "pity" whispered along the fringes of his consciousness. It grew larger, floating upward like a scrap of paper being raised by the wind. He shook himself free of it.

"My car's right there." Raven pointed toward the lot at a sleek red sports car that sat low to the ground. "You can follow me."

"Follow you?" He wasn't even following her mentally and had no intentions of doing so physically.

She turned, looking up at him again. "Home, so you can tell Blue."

He'd assumed that suggestion had faded away. "I thought that we—that I—"

To Peter's surprise, Raven lightly touched his cheek, silencing him as the sensation undulated through him, rolling along his flesh.

Raven raised her eyes to his and smiled.

He could feel that very same smile unfurling inside his chest, as if, for just a single moment in time, they were one, sharing a single action. "We did," she told him, her voice low.

Obviously her "we did" was different than his, Peter thought.

What did it matter? There were still a number of hours left before midnight and he never fell asleep before then. Sometimes not even then.

Peter shrugged, surrendering the small battle, not wanting to waste his energy on it. Moving away from the front entrance, he took a couple of steps toward the car she'd pointed out to get a closer look at it.

His eyebrows pulled together. No, his eyes weren't playing tricks on him. He looked down at Raven. "A Ferrari?"

"You sound surprised."

He supposed he was at that. "I guess I pictured you driving around in a VW bus."

He tried not to notice the appealing grin that curved her mouth. "Complete with flowers painted on the side?"

Ordinarily he would have said that she was laughing at him. Except that he couldn't feel himself taking offense. Her expression was too genial, too deliciously amused.

"Yes," he conceded.

He watched a shimmer of delight brightening eyes the color of a cloudless, midmorning sky.

"Actually, that was my parents' vehicle—and where my mother ultimately began her company." She pulled her expression into a serious one, and almost succeeded. "But driving around in something that vintage now would be kind of unsafe, don't you think?"

His eyes swept over her. It was like carrying on a conversation with pixie dust. Glittery, shimmery, but if he tried to catch hold of it, there would be nothing in his hands. "I got the impression you didn't trouble yourself with things like that."

Again the laugh—musical, light—went right through him, embedding itself within his marrow. "You have a lot to learn about me, Peter."

Peter. Not Dr. Sullivan, or even just Doctor, but Peter. The structure he'd built up so carefully all around him was being torn away with her delicate, bare hands. And again, she was talking as if this was the beginning of a relationship instead of something that was meant, by design, to be quick, fleeting. Over with before it ever really got started.

"You know," she was saying after she'd allowed her words to sink in, "I've always loved the color red and I've loved Ferraris ever since I saw Tom Selleck fold his muscular body up into one on *Magnum P.I.*"

"You watched television?" Something else he couldn't visualize her doing.

She could almost read the thoughts as they telegraphed themselves into his head. "Children of neo-hippies got to watch television." She laughed.

And then she leaned her head into his, as if about to impart some deep, dark secret only he could hear. The scent of wildflowers and honeysuckle penetrated his consciousness, filling his head even though, logically, the night air should have easily dissipated it. But apparently logic and Raven Songbird could not coexist in the same space.

"Besides, I saw the show on one of the cable

channels. Burned the whole series onto DVD disks,'' she confided with a wink.

He had no idea what she was trying to convey with the wink, only that it went through him with the force of a bullet hitting its target dead center.

What the hell was going on here? he wondered. Was he coming down with something? During all his years at medical school and in residency, surrounded by sick people, he'd never come down with so much as a cold. It looked as if his luck had run out.

''Never saw it myself,'' he muttered when she continued to look at him as if he should know what she was talking about.

He thought that would put her off. Even at this point, he realized he should have known better. Nothing seemed to put her off. She was like one of those little yellow toy ducks that bobbed upright no matter how hard you tried to sink it.

''No?'' Her eyes widened. ''Then you're in for a treat. It had everything—humor, action, mystery, buddies being there for each other, terrific scenery. Anytime you're up for it,'' she impulsively promised, ''we can make a marathon of it.''

Assaulted with her enthusiasm, his head was beginning to spin. ''Excuse me?''

''A marathon,'' she repeated. ''You know, the way they do on some of the cable networks whenever there's some kind of a holiday. Ten, twelve uninterrupted hours of something or other,'' she prompted when he continued to look at her as if she'd suddenly begun spouting Martian. ''In this case, *Magnum.*''

He had absolutely no intention of sitting anywhere with her, watching anything. The scenario she was suggesting was far too intimate. It was something he and Lisa had done. ''Wasting time'' someone on the outside would have called it. Savoring time was the way he saw it.

''I've never had ten uninterrupted hours of something, other than work,'' he amended. His tone was meant to cut the conversation dead.

But it refused to die. ''Might be just what the doctor ordered.''

Peter frowned. He'd once been told that his frown could freeze a sunspot at fifty paces. ''Not this doctor.''

Unfazed, Raven was devoid of any frostbite. Instead, there was actual concern on her face as she gazed up at him. ''Why are you trying so hard to be superhuman? To deny that you *can* be human?''

Maybe it was because he was warming up to her and maybe, here in the darkness, he allowed himself a rare moment of truth, a rare moment in which he allowed the truth to be heard by a complete stranger. A very strange stranger. ''Because being human is extremely painful, extremely unrewarding and if I wasn't attempting to be 'superhuman' as you call it, your brother might not stand any chance at all to—"

Peter never got a chance to finish what he was trying to say.

One moment he was lecturing this woman who had exploded into his life. The very next moment, his lips were no longer moving. Or at least, no longer allowing any sounds to slip past them.

They were sealed to hers.

It happened so suddenly, Peter had no idea how he'd gotten from point A to point B. For a moment he entertained the idea that he was either hallucinating or having, quite possibly, an out-of-body experience. One moment, only darkness surrounded him, and the next, bright lights went off, filling him inside and enveloping him on the outside.

Lights and warmth and something that he vaguely recognized as desire.

Which was impossible. Because desire in all forms had deserted him. Whether it encompassed the most basic kind or just a craving for a particular food, he had become utterly devoid of it.

Until now.

He felt desire, robust and full-bodied.

He would have sworn this part of him had died at Lisa's gravesite. He'd become, for all intents and purposes, a hollow man.

Yet he wanted to be kissing this woman he'd inexplicably found his lips pressed against. Wanted to be holding her to him, feeling her soft, supple body molding into his.

Wanted this rush that both hurt and felt good.

He was coming unglued.

She knew it, knew that it would be like this. Knew the second she had seen the tall, dark, brooding doctor and heard his voice. Knew that there was trapped emotion within him that if she could only tap, would sweep her away.

And she needed to be swept away, needed to feel, just for a moment, as if every star in the universe was in the right place and that everything, *everything* would be all right.

Anything less was unthinkable.

She needed to know, to be convinced, that this man cared. Because only a caring man could fix her brother and make him well again.

Raven raised herself up on her toes, her fingertips digging into a pair of strong, muscular shoulders. It was hard to remain grounded when all the forces of the known world conspired to make her let go and just be, just feel.

A sigh escaped her.

It had been a very, very long time since she'd allowed herself this kind of a connection. In her own way, she was as removed as the doctor she was trying to bring around. She hadn't lost a soul mate, but she had lost pieces of her soul. Her parents had been very precious to her and the irony that they had died while on their way to see her moment of triumph was not lost on her. It brought with it a vast amount of guilt.

She tried to assuage her guilt by being both mother and father to Blue. And by running the company that her parents had started. It was their legacy, as was Blue, and neither was going to be allowed to be anything less than perfect in every way.

It kept her from making any deeply personal connections. Not the kind that would ultimately result in her having a home and family of her own. She had the memory of receiving her diploma, then being taken aside by a teacher and told that two-thirds of her family had died and that the little brother she adored was fighting for his life. This memory kept her from making any more commitments.

But this wasn't a commitment. This was something different.

For a moment longer she allowed the kiss to deepen, allowed the sensation to quicken every pulse in her body. And then, because she knew that if it went on even a breath longer, she might not be able to regain her footing, might not be able to stand, much less think clearly, Raven pulled back.

Her heart was hammering so hard, she was ninety-eight percent certain it would lodge itself in her throat, preventing her from talking. She cleared her throat for just that reason, to make sure she still could.

She'd kissed him.

The thought throbbed through his brain as more and more functioning parts returned. He struggled to keep them from floating away again.

"Why did you do that?" he asked, looking at her. "Why did you kiss me?"

"Because you needed me to," she replied without blinking an eye. Inside, there were banked questions of her own. Questions such as, Had he been as affected by the kiss as she had? Had the world trembled for him the way it had for her? Or had the strain of worrying about Blue, about what could happen to her brother if things went wrong, finally made her crack?

"I need you to?" He stared at her. "What are you talking about?"

"You seemed so alone—"

He gestured toward her impatiently. "I was standing here with you."

"You can be in the middle of a crowd and still be alone."

He didn't like the fact that she was playing Gypsy fortune-teller with him. Worse, he didn't like the fact that she seemed to be reading him so well. Because she was right on target, which was waging hell on his resolution to keep his distance from the world at large. He wasn't about to let any of it in, ever. The price was too high.

And what he hated most of all was that the desire to take her back into his arms, to kiss her again with the same feeling, the same passion he just experienced, was still alive, still thriving in his veins, urging him on.

He shrouded himself in anger. It was the only weapon he had.

"I don't need to be psychoanalyzed, Raven." Because she'd unsettled so much inside of him, he glared at her. "We'll get along a lot better if you keep that in mind."

"It wasn't a matter of psychoanalyzing you," she told him gently. "It was more a case of one kindred soul connecting with another."

"And that's how you connect?"

She gave a half shrug, one shoulder rising, brushing against her hair. "Beats paper clips."

She'd called them kindred souls. He was no more like her than he was like a mermaid. Trying to get a grip on his thoughts, he shook his head and laughed dryly. "You really are something else, aren't you?"

The trouble was, he was beginning to suspect that he didn't know what that something else was. He didn't like the unknown.

Not answering him, Raven watched him for a long moment. "So," she finally said, getting back to her original subject, "will you come to the house and tell Blue?"

The light dawned. She'd tried to entice him. "Was that what the kiss was about? To make sure I'd come talk to your brother?"

If he expected her to look guilty or embarrassed at being caught, he was disappointed. She appeared to be neither.

"No. That was strictly about you. And maybe a little about me," she allowed. "You're not some adolescent to be coerced into doing something because someone kissed you." Raven paused for a second, as if weighing something in her mind. "If you don't feel up to it, I'll tell him myself. It's just that I think he'd rather hear it coming from you."

Peter watched the wind ripple through her hair, playing with strands before moving on. She had let him off the hook. The woman knew just how to maneuver, he thought. She would have made a hell of a general. "Give me a few minutes to get to my car," he told her. "Then you can go ahead and lead the way to your house."

Turning on his heel, he still didn't miss the smile that came to her lips. It almost made the capitulation worth it.

Chapter Six

Obviously not all neo-hippies took a vow of poverty, Peter thought as he approached the place where Raven lived. He'd seen smaller, less impressive castles. The driveway was comprised of countless tiny, colored rocks that were arranged to form the company's logo—a white dove soaring through a crystal-blue sky. He almost hated parking his vehicle on it.

She was out of her car and at his side before he had a chance to close his door. There was pleasure and more than a hint of surprise on her face.

"I didn't think you'd follow me all the way," she confessed. "I kept looking in the rearview mirror to see if you'd suddenly decided to make good your escape.'' She sounded as if she was only half kidding.

''It crossed my mind,'' Peter conceded.

Despite the nip in the air, she'd driven her car with the top down. He had to admit that the sight of her hair whipping around as she drove had been a compelling, enticing picture.

But her hair wasn't why he'd followed her. Once he said he would do something, he kept his word. Without a family to mark his passage, Peter felt that his word was all he had. His word and his work. He meant for both to stand for something.

She flashed a grin. ''Glad it was only passing through.''

Taking his hand as if they were old friends instead of two people who didn't know each other a few days ago, Raven led him to the front door. She glanced over her shoulder to see his reaction and nodded in silent agreement when she caught his eye.

''It's a little over the top,'' she allowed. ''My father bought it for my mother the day she told him she was pregnant with Blue. He wanted to do something spectacular for her.'' Fond memories left their mark upon her features as she remembered. ''He cried when she first told him, he was so happy. Said there was no greater miracle than a baby.''

''No,'' Peter agreed quietly, thinking of Becky,

remembering how he'd felt the first time he'd held her in his hands, ''there isn't.''

He was rewarded with a smile that went straight to his gut, as if fired from a high-powered rifle. He really wished she'd stop doing that, stop detonating all these small land mines inside of him. It was getting in the way of his thinking.

''Isn't he asleep?'' Peter asked, realizing that while it was early for him, a child of seven might very well already be tucked into bed.

She laughed and shook her head. For a while, bedtime had been an issue between them, but then she'd decided to raise him the way her parents had raised her, by giving Blue his own head in the matter.

''Not yet,'' she assured Peter. ''He doesn't really seem to need much sleep and he likes to stay up with me, so most nights, I let him fall asleep on his own and then just carry him off to bed.''

That sounded more in keeping with the lifestyle he attributed to someone like her. The thought vaguely amused him because he'd never really known anyone quite like Raven and her bohemian way of life. His own life had been strictly regimented. Growing up without a mother, the only parenting skills he'd known were his father's. Larry Sullivan was a former Marine turned dock worker whose entire life ran on discipline and punctuality. Other things, such as love, never entered into the mix. He felt his mother died because it was the only way she could get away from his father.

Peter caught himself watching how Raven's hips swayed gently as she walked across a blue-and-white marble foyer.

"I'm home," she called. Her voice seemed to echo up the wide spiral staircase.

A middle-aged woman with thin ribbons of gray running through her jet-black hair came from the rear of the house. Her face was round and perfect for the warm, genial expression she wore.

"He's in the media room, Raven."

"Thank you, Connie." About to dash off, Raven halted in midstride, remembering that these two did not know one another. She gestured from one to the other. "Oh, Consuela, Peter. Peter, Consuela."

The woman inclined her head. It was obvious that the dark eyes were taking complete and strict measure of him, despite the friendly smile on her face. Consuela nodded acknowledgment, then continued on her way to the kitchen.

"Connie looks out for Blue when I'm not around and kind of keeps up on things for me. She's been with us forever," Raven told him as she led the way to the back of the house. And then, because it was important to Connie, even though she was no longer within earshot, she added, "She used to play backup for a band."

"Of course she did," he muttered. At this point,

Peter was beginning to feel that he would believe almost anything Raven told him. Coming here to this house was not unlike stepping through the looking glass. Instead of rabbits hurrying by with pocket watches in their hands, there were aging rockers.

But the evening was young. The rabbit might still turn up.

Raven opened a door just off the family room and gave him his first peek into the media room. It looked exactly like a miniature movie theater, complete with tiered theater seats arranged in rows of four. Twenty seats in all faced the largest screen he'd seen outside of a movie house.

Maybe inside of a few, too.

Raven read his expression. She inclined her head toward his, whispering in his ear so as not to interfere with the on-screen dialogue. ''Dad wanted to make it three times this size, but Mom liked things cozy.''

Cozy was definitely not the first word that would have popped into his head. Unless it had to do with the person at his side.

''Right,'' Peter responded after a beat, pulling himself back from the wave of heat traveling through him thanks to her proximity and the effect her warm breath drifting along his skin had on him. Being around her was making a jumble of his thought process.

His antenna going up, the lone figure in the first

row turned around and saw them. The beatific smile instantly spread along his small lips. Without a second thought, Blue abandoned the movie he was watching. He rushed back to where they stood.

"Dr. Pete, you're here."

The boy was way too informal for him, Peter thought. But at least Blue attached the title of "Dr." to his greeting, which was more than Raven had done when she'd introduced him to her housekeeper.

He glanced toward Raven. It was as if everything about her was trying to strip away the insulating layers he kept around himself, the ones that kept him safe from the rest of the world. From the pain that he kept at bay 24/7, every single moment of his life. Kept at bay until such time as it wouldn't eat him alive.

That time hadn't come yet.

Blue still beamed at him. "Raven said she'd bring you by."

Obviously the woman didn't have a drop of humility in her. And she seemed to run completely on confidence. He eyed her now, knowing he should have been annoyed at being taken for granted this way. But for some reason the ire didn't come.

"Oh, she did, did she?"

Raven shrugged out of her pea coat, leaving it slung across the back of one of the seats. "I had a hunch you wouldn't say no."

Hunch. So that was what she called her brand of arrogance? Peter couldn't help wondering just what lengths she would have ultimately gone to, to get him to come along so that she could continue to look like the heroine to her brother. She might appear like something that would be found floating along on a warm summer night's breeze, but he was getting the definite feeling that the lady was as tough as nails.

An iron butterfly. That was probably the best way to describe her.

Climbing up on a seat in the last row, Blue winced ever so slightly before straightening. The action was not lost on Peter. Most children the boy's age would have whimpered and begun to cry, complaining of the pain he knew Blue had to be experiencing. Yet the child in front of him seemed determined to tough it out. Brother and sister had a lot in common, he thought. For one thing, they were both stubborn as hell.

There were worse traits to have.

Blue looked at him eagerly. "What?" he asked. "When are you going to fix me?"

Peter cleared his throat. "I'm afraid it's not that simple."

No, don't go into it, don't start explaining, Raven thought, suddenly worried.

"If you boil away all the explanations, it is," Raven told him cheerfully as she interrupted anything he might have had to say. She gave him a warning look that clearly told him not to go into any kind of elaborate detail, especially none concerning the odds and the possible downsides of the surgery. She forged ahead to the one question on her brother's mind. "How soon can you schedule him?"

Peter looked at her for a long moment. He wanted to give her one last chance to back out. "You're certain?" he asked. He was fairly sure she hadn't examined the matter closely, other than deciding to go full steam ahead.

Raven exchanged looks with her brother and then took the boy's hand in hers. "We're certain, right, Blue?"

"Right." Blue looked straight at him as he made the declaration.

Maybe he was just overtired, but it didn't sound to him as if the boy was parroting his sister. Instead it was as if he was just echoing his own feelings on the subject. Blue seemed to have had a hand in making the choice to go ahead with his surgery.

But if Blue was clear about what he wanted, Peter still had misgivings. *Did* the boy truly understand what was at stake? Did he know the possible outcome of the surgery if it wasn't one hundred percent successful? Or even if it was, even if he removed all the tumors, other things could go wrong.

But he'd done his talking to Raven and he

couldn't say anything to Blue. It was too much to lay on a small boy's shoulders.

Peter suppressed a sigh. This situation brought home how much he didn't like having children as his patients. It was bad enough having in his mind the specter of what could possibly happen when he operated on an adult. A child had an entire lifetime shimmering ahead of him. A lifetime that might not be lived or enjoyed.

Just as Becky had never gotten to live hers. The thought came out of nowhere, assaulting him. Wounding him.

Raven immediately saw the change in his expression. He looked as if he was in pain. She placed her hand on his arm, calling his attention away from whatever it was that was doing this to him. "What's the matter?"

He shook the thought, the moment, away. He had no idea why, but taking on this case had become much too personal for him.

Peter looked at her blankly. "What?"

"You have an odd expression on your face." It was gone now, but she knew that whatever he'd been thinking had upset him. "Can I get you something?"

Yes, get me my life back. Get me back the life I lost. It's not fair, not fair to let me see what I could have and then to take it away from me in a blink of an eye.

He straightened his shoulders. ''No,'' he told her quietly. ''I was just thinking how unusually mature your brother sounds.'' It was a good lie, he thought, and it fit the moment.

Blue raised himself up on his toes, as if that could help him grow the added inch. He grinned at the unintentional compliment.

''Gets it from me, don't you, puppy?'' Raven laughed, tousling her brother's hair. In response, the boy giggled and suddenly sounded the way a seven-year-old should. Gleeful and happy.

At that moment something prompted Peter to make a silent promise that the boy was going to have his childhood unencumbered by a wheelchair. Peter focused on this promise as it became, for the time being, his one sole reason for living.

His eyes shifted toward Raven. ''Call me tomorrow morning,'' he instructed her. ''We'll schedule his surgery then.''

Blue moved in front of him, blocking his exit. ''As soon as possible?''

The pain had to be getting to him, Peter realized. No one willingly embraced the idea of surgery unless they were in the throes of pain and felt there was no alternative.

Awkwardly, he laid his hand on the boy's shoulder, fleetingly connecting with him. ''As soon as possible,'' Peter echoed.

There were too many feelings here; too much going on. He needed to clear his head, to find some solitude. Peter began to back away. But he should have known that the perfect getaway was not within his reach, not with Raven anywhere in the vicinity.

Abandoning the media room, she blocked his path. "You can hang around and watch Roger Rabbit," she offered, nodding back into the media room. She laughed at the expression on his face. "Or make your own selection. We've got an entire library of movies."

He sidestepped her, only to be blocked again. "I don't really watch movies," he told Raven. "Not enough time."

"That's the beauty of DVDs and tapes," she told him as she threaded her arm through his. Out of the corner of his eye, he saw Blue return and settle back into his front row seat to watch the rest of the movie. To his surprise, Raven began walking toward the front of the house, as if she already knew that he wasn't going to be talked into remaining tonight. "You can stop anytime you want to and then resume watching whenever you get the chance."

"Maybe some other time," he told her.

"Okay." Very slowly, she withdrew her arm. He was acutely aware of how every inch of it rubbed along his arm. Though he wore a jacket, he could still feel her. "I'll hold you to that."

With a sigh, he stopped at the front door.

"Why?" he asked. "Why would you hold me to that? Why do you want me to watch Magnum Detective—"

"'Magnum P.I.,'" she corrected, doing her best not to laugh at him.

He took no offense at the laughter in her eyes. What worried the hell out of him was the sudden, almost overpowering urge to sweep her into his arms and kiss her. He just didn't behave that way. And even if he'd *ever* been that way, everything was different now in this solitary world he'd dwelt in since Lisa's death. He *couldn't* feel that way about anyone else.

What the hell was happening to him, anyway?

"That—" He waved his hand impatiently at the title she'd just supplied, feeling like a man on the brink of insanity. "Why are you trying to carve a niche into my life?" He realized he was shouting.

If he'd meant to intimidate her, he'd failed. Nothing blunted the look of compassion in her eyes. And maybe that was the worst part of all. Compassion was synonymous with pity in his mind and he didn't want her pity, didn't want anyone's pity. He just wanted to continue as he had, separate from everyone.

"Because you look like you could use a friend, Peter," she explained quietly. "You know that old saying, if you see someone without a smile, give him one of yours—"

"No, I don't know that old saying." He bit the words off impatiently.

She only smiled. "Well, there is one, trust me. And if I ever saw someone who needed a smile, or a friend, I'd say it was you."

Damn it, he didn't need a do-gooder. He needed to be left alone, to do the work he could and just go on, nothing more, nothing less. He glared at this woman who was burrowing a hole into his life. "And what's in it for you?"

Her answer came without any hesitation. "A friend, I hope."

The simple statement ripped into him. "You're serious." He stared at her.

"Sure. Why wouldn't I be?"

Was she for real? Didn't those parents of hers teach her anything while wandering around the country? Didn't their *deaths* teach her anything?

"Because people just don't act that way."

Two small words completely negated the point he was trying to make. "I do."

Peter shook the head that she was so completely messing with. He didn't understand her. But then, he supposed he didn't have to. All he had to do was to operate on her brother and then move on, the way he'd always done before. A few weeks from now, this would all be a blur in the past.

He opened the door and glanced at her. "Call my office tomorrow."

Her eyes held his until he managed to pull them away. "I'd rather come by."

He had to remain firm on this. Capitulating would only jeopardize his ability to focus. "And I'd rather you called."

To his surprise, she let him get the last word in. At least, he didn't hear any coming from her as she closed the door behind him.

He felt oddly hollow again. But then, it was a familiar feeling.

He couldn't help but feel uptight, invaded. Unsettled.

It made no sense to him. Raven Songbird was, after all, just a slip of a thing. One lone woman in a sea of people who flowed in and out of his offices within the year. Why was she lingering on his mind like the lyrics of a song that refused to fade away?

He had no answer for that. All he did was continue to feel unwanted sensations all through the night. They accompanied him to the hospital the next morning, giving no indication of leaving anytime soon.

Supported by a minimum amount of sleep he was still trying to sort it all out when George Grissom walked into his office after one short, perfunctory knock. There was no greeting, no preamble as the six-foot-five hospital administrator entered, ducking his head under the doorway. ''I had no idea you were operating on the Songbird boy.''

Peter turned from his desk, surprised. Was his entire life on the Internet these days? ''Until yesterday, I wasn't. I haven't even called to schedule yet. How did you find out?''

''Because Raven Songbird just called to say she was writing a sizable check to the hospital so that we could get another one of those full-body scanners, not to mention several other pieces of cutting-edge equipment we've had our eye on.'' He looked at Peter with admiration. ''She said it was because she was grateful that you've decided to operate on her brother.''

She was doing it so that he wouldn't suddenly decide to change his mind and back out, Peter thought. In effect, she had him surrounded, bringing in reinforcements in the guise of a very vocal, very dedicated hospital administrator. Grissom liked nothing better than receiving donations he hadn't had to break his back to get.

Peter took his hat off to her even as she annoyed him.

''I haven't checked to see when the next available slot is,'' Peter informed him. It was just past eight. The scheduling office wouldn't be open for another half hour.

''Any time she wants,'' George informed him. ''I want her treated with kid gloves,'' he emphasized.

''Her parents donated the entire cancer wing to the hospital. I'm glad to see that she's going to be carrying on in their memory. You're to do nothing to make her change her mind.''

Peter swung his chair around to face the administrator. He took offense at the implication he perceived. ''What, like operate at a level that's other than my best?''

The scowl on the florid face told him that George was offended by the implication. ''You know I didn't mean that, Peter. I was talking about your less than charming bedside manner.''

Peter blew out a breath. ''You're too late. I've already tried it out on the woman. I'm sorry to say it had no effect on her. She continued to come on like gangbusters.''

George shook his head. ''And my wife wonders why I'm gray.''

''You were born gray, George,'' Peter quipped as the man left his office again.

He turned back around to his desk. At least George had a wife, he thought darkly.

Pulling back from the thought before it could drag him down to the tarry depths of depression, Peter began to go over his schedule.

Chapter Seven

It wasn't Peter's custom to stop by a patient's room just before surgery. As a rule, the last time he would see a patient before surgery would be on the day the arrangements were made and the surgery was scheduled. There would be a desk between them and antiseptic words to help preserve the distance he liked to maintain.

In all the time that he had been a surgeon, he'd never acquired that comforting manner of glad-handing someone, of standing next to their bedside and assuring them that everything would be all right. It wasn't within his power to give those kinds of guarantees. He would do the very best he could, that was understood. It was a tacit given that he didn't feel he had to repeat.

However, there were things that went beyond his control, things that happened in a realm that defied rhyme, or reason, or the very best of precautions. Those "things" fell under the unnerving heading of Chance or Fate. Or whatever it was that explained the occurrence, to some degree, to the patient and/or to his or her family.

It wasn't up to him to dip into that. His function was to use the best of his skills, honed and perfected with each operation he'd performed, or assisted with, or watched. He used his skills to do the impossible, or at least, whatever he could to correct what was wrong. He was a body mechanic, pure and simple.

So he was more than a little surprised to discover that the steps he took from his hospital office did not lead him directly to the third-floor operating salon. Instead, they led him to the first floor, taking him past the reception area to the tiny rooms that were grouped under the all-encompassing title of "Pre-op."

It was here, to these cheery-looking, sun-drenched rooms that patients were taken before their operations. They were asked to abandon their own clothing and to don breezy one-size-fits-all gowns that ultimately made them seem like an assembly line product. These products would be worked upon for a measure of time, then set aside as the next assembly line item came down the conveyor belt. All in all, it was a rather dehumanizing process, but that was the way he liked it. He performed best at a distance.

He was operating on Blue today.

Less than a week had gone by since the boy had first popped his head into the office, asking him if he was God. Five days to be exact.

He felt as if it had been longer.

Normally he had no feelings one way or another about patients. What usually filled every part of him was a determination to do the best he could. To "fix" them, as Blue had put it.

This time, no matter how much he tried to pretend that there weren't, there were feelings. That was the boy's doing.

The boy's and his sister's.

Was he God? Blue's question echoed in his brain. He knew that he'd never felt as if he were God. Unlike some neurosurgeons who believed that they walked a little above all the other surgeons, he had never felt that way, never felt as if there was the slightest bit of deity within him.

He was the most ungodlike creature to have ever walked the earth.

But if there was any truth to the notion that neurosurgeons were the right hand of God, then he hoped it would be true today, for the length of time that it took to complete Blue's operation. He freely, if silently, admitted that he would need help today. Because this surgery was going to be as delicate as they came.

The boy was small for his age. Peter knew without reviewing his records that he had never operated on anyone younger than eighteen before and even the most diminutive of his patients did not hold a candle to Blue.

Peter looked down at his hands. For the first time since his first year in surgery, he wondered if his fingers were skilled enough. If they were perhaps too large for the task.

That was what feeling got you, he thought in annoyance. Doubts. Doubts that could get in the way.

The door in front of him opened. A young, male lab technician emerged from the room. He was holding a tray in his hands that contained fresh samples of the boy's blood.

Thrown off, the technician, whose name tag proclaimed him to be Javier, did a little sidestep, trying to get out of his way but managing only to block his every move. Flashing a sheepish grin, the technician took one more large step to finally get out of his way.

"Sorry," Javier mumbled into his chin as he hurried away.

Putting out his hand to keep the door from closing again, Peter grunted something in response.

The room only had one occupied bed. Grissom at work, Peter thought. In his desire to cull their continuing favor, George had seen to it that Blue was given a private pre-op room rather than having to share the space with five other people scheduled for surgery around the same time, the way normal procedure dictated.

Peter breathed a small sigh of relief. He didn't care for crowds.

Framed by the early morning sun that pressed itself through the window behind her, Raven stood by her brother's bed, holding Blue's hand in hers. She murmured something to the boy Peter couldn't quite make out. It took effort for him not to stare at her, transfixed.

Both Raven and Blue looked at him as he crossed the threshold. The door closed softly behind him, as if nothing on this side of the hospital could make a loud noise.

Raven seemed relieved to see him. She gestured toward him with her free hand. ''And here he is now. See? I told you he'd stop by before you went in,'' Raven said to her brother.

The woman knew more than he did, Peter thought.

Moving closer to the bed, he noticed that her face was just the slightest bit drawn, as if she were struggling to stay brave. For the most part, she was winning, but there was just a hint of turmoil evident beneath the surface. Raven Songbird was deeply worried about her brother.

Nodding at Raven, Peter looked at the boy who sat propped up in the bed. Meant for adults, the bed succeeded in dwarfing him, making him appear even smaller than he was.

He addressed Blue the way he would any of his adult patients. He sensed the boy expected that. Welcomed that. "How are you doing?"

Blue sat up a little straighter. "Okay." It was obvious that the boy tried very hard to put on as brave a front as his sister had.

"They just came to cross match his blood. Took a whole bunch of it from him and he didn't even cry, did you, Tiger?" Raven affectionately feathered her fingers through her brother's black hair. Every movement, every look, showed Peter how proud she was of the boy.

Blue merely moved his head from side to side. "I don't cry," the boy told him solemnly.

Peter raised his eyes to look at Raven. "Ever?"

"No, he doesn't," she said. At times, this worried her, but for the most part, Blue was a source of never-ending sunshine in her life and she felt blessed.

Peter could only shake his head in wonder. "My father would have loved having you."

The personal revelation surprised her. And gave her just a sprinkling of hope. Some of the biggest battles were won an inch at a time. The word ''battles'' linked up with another and she looked at Peter.

''Was your father a Marine?''

She hadn't even bothered with the nebulous term of ''soldier.'' He would have, presented with the same evidence.

Picking up Blue's chart, he quickly scanned it, then returned it to where it was hanging from the end of the bed. ''How did you know?''

She shrugged. The neckline that was all too wide slipped from her shoulder. She pushed it back into place. ''Lucky guess.''

He forced his eyes away from the creamy white expanse of her neck and shoulders. Looking into her eyes was no improvement. They were much too blue, made him drift and lose focus. He couldn't afford that right now.

Couldn't afford it at any time.

He turned his attention back to Blue and dispensed a little more information for the boy's benefit. ''After this is over, you're going to have to lie on your stomach for about a week.'' Most kids would probably balk at remaining immobilized that way, he thought.

Blue merely nodded his head. ''I know.''

He sounded like someone four times his age, Peter thought. ''How do you know?''

Blue's eyes shifted toward his sister. ''Raven told me.''

Leaning against the raised side railing, Peter transferred his question. ''All right, I'll bite, how did you know?''

''I've been doing a lot of reading up on the subject,'' she told him. Optimistic though she might be, there was no way she was going to blindly allow anything to be done to her brother without first knowing every single ramification involved.

Peter nodded his approval.

Behind them, the door opened and a matronly looking nurse entered. ''I've got to give him his medication,'' she told Raven before flashing an encouraging smile at Blue. ''It's going to help you fall asleep.''

Looking almost like a little old man, resigned to his fate, Blue put out his bare arm, waiting for the inevitable sting of a needle. The nurse laughed. She held out a little white cup. Inside was a tiny yellow pill. ''No, this you swallow.''

Blue's face immediately brightened. ''Good.'' His eyes shifted toward his doctor. ''I really hate shots,'' he confided.

Peter merely nodded. ''Not my favorite thing, either,'' he allowed. He glanced at his watch. It was almost time. He had to get upstairs to prepare. ''I'll see you in surgery.''

''Okay,'' Blue called after him.

Raven caught up to him just before he went through the door. ''Where's the chapel?'' she asked, almost breathless. It was as if the impact of what was about to unfold was hitting her. He fought the urge to comfort her.

''It's just outside the Intensive Care Unit,'' he told her.

''Appropriate,'' he heard her murmur as she withdrew to join her brother.

Funny, all this time, he'd never thought of that before.

If she knotted her fingers together any tighter, she might never untangle them. Raven could feel her heart pounding inside her chest, threatening to break out. She didn't know how much more of this she could take.

The surgery was running longer than it should have. Much longer.

In trying to prepare for everything, she'd consulted three different medical books as to the procedure and the length of time that it would take. Given the nature and location of the tumors, the consensus was that the surgery should take approximately four hours.

More than five had passed.

She tried to tell herself not to worry, that Peter was just being careful. The surgery wasn't something to race through and she was sure he wouldn't try to beat his best time. He was taking precautions, just like any good surgeon would. Wasn't that why she'd come to Sullivan in the first place? Because he was good? Because his reputation was excellent?

She could feel tears filling her eyes. It wasn't the first time. She blinked them away.

Concern continued to nag at her, growing larger and more unwieldy as each minute passed. She looked at the big clock on the wall at the end of the corridor. Each second dragged by.

It was taking too long.

The words echoed in her brain like some kind of a warning. A premonition of dire things to come.

She was making herself crazy.

What if something had gone wrong? What if Blue was paralyzed and Peter didn't know how to come out to tell her? No, he'd tell her. He'd do it the way they ripped off Band-Aids, in one swift movement.

What if they'd sent the tissues to be analyzed at the lab and had gotten back a result that pronounced the tumors to be malignant?

Her mind raced from one dark scenario to another, each one more terrifying than the last. She struggled vainly to get her thoughts back in balance.

Why weren't her parents here? She needed them here with her to make this bearable.

Her parents had always taught her to have a good outlook about everything, to see the positive side. But her parents were gone, taken from her just as she was about to embark on her first real journey of consequence. Sending her entire life veering off in a completely different direction. One moment she was a young woman with a supportive family and the whole world open to her, the next she was an orphan. An orphan with a two-year-old to take care of.

Not only that, but she'd suddenly inherited her parents' company, something she was only familiar with in the most cursory of ways. Overnight over a thousand people were counting on her for their very livelihood. It had been a hell of a thing to be saddled with at twenty-two.

This was worse.

Waiting to find out what was going on in the operating room less than a hundred feet away was undoing her.

She had begun the vigil by going into the chapel to pray. That had lasted for a little less than an hour. Feeling as if she'd worn out her knees, she'd gone to the visitors' lounge to wait for news. But there were too many people there, talking, laughing, trying to distract one another. Being around them just made her edgy. She'd remained in the lounge as long as she could, then left.

Taking the elevator, she'd returned to the third floor, where Peter was holding her brother's fate in his hands. She followed the signs to the operating room and for the past hour she'd been out here in the hall, standing or pacing—waiting.

Life around her moved in slow motion, as if it belonged to another universe that only marginally touched her own.

The hospital personnel who walked by looked at her curiously. One of the orderlies stopped to ask her if she was lost. She shook her head, demurring.

But she felt lost. Lost and alone.

This'll pass, she promised herself silently. Raven only prayed she was right.

What if? kept echoing in her brain.

As the sixth hour approached, she had lost track of the amount of deals she'd made with God. Deals that hinged on some kind of sacrifice on her part if only He'd let Blue come out of this surgery alive and well.

Pacing from one end of the hall to the other, her feet gained momentum as her concern mounted. It escalated until she was almost a swirl of color. And each time she passed the double doors through which her brother had been taken, she stared, willing them to open. Willing the surgeon she'd placed her faith in to come out and tell her that everything was all right. That there was no need to worry like this.

The doors remained closed.

Her agitation increased.

As she turned away for the umpteenth time from

the doors, she walked directly into George Grissom, hitting her face against his massive chest.

The big man took a step back, as if alarmed that he had hurt her. ''Are you all right?''

Numb not from the encounter, but from worry, Raven was aware of nodding. ''As well as can be expected. He's still in there.'' The words came out in a whisper.

The hospital administrator eyed her nervously. It was obvious that he'd been looking for her. ''Ms. Songbird, what are you doing here?''

She blew out a long, ragged breath, looking at the closed doors accusingly. ''Waiting.''

''Yes, I understand.'' He began to take her arm to direct her toward the elevator. ''But wouldn't you be more comfortable downstairs in the visitors' lounge?''

Comfortable was not a word that meant anything to her anymore. ''I was there for four hours, Mr. Grissom. I couldn't stay there any longer. And right now, I don't think I could be comfortable anywhere.''

His expression was understanding as he nodded. ''He's one of the best neurosurgeons in the country.''

''I know.'' That was the only reason she wasn't crawling out of her skin by now. But she was getting close.

"Perhaps you'd like to have something to eat?" George suggested hopefully. "We could—"

Shaking her head, she pulled back. "No, thank you. Really." The smile she offered was grateful but firm. "I understand that you're trying to get my mind off what's happening in there, but you can't." And then she paused, thinking. "But there is maybe something that you can do for me."

"Name it."

"Is there any way to call in there to find out if everything—" Her voice hitched. She tried again. "If everything's all right?"

"There is a phone in the operating room," he acknowledged, although his expression told her that he doubted the wisdom of calling right now. She knew she was being impatient, but after nearly six hours, she felt as if she was coming perilously close to falling apart.

Sympathy entered George's deep gray eyes. He looked around for the nearest phone. "Why don't we go to the nurse's station and..."

Whatever he was about to suggest faded away unsaid. The outer doors to the operating salon opened before he could finish. A tall man dressed completely in green livery walked out, his face still covered with a surgical mask.

She would have recognized his eyes anywhere.

Raven was at Peter's side in less than a heartbeat,

firing questions at him before he could even strip away his mask.

"Is he all right? Is Blue going to make it? Will he be able to walk?"

Peter felt drained. He'd performed longer surgeries, but none that had ever mattered as much to him as this one had. The sensation still mystified him. He didn't like feeling as if he had everything riding on the outcome of a surgery. In his opinion, that only impeded his skills and could wind up jeopardizing the whole outcome.

But he hadn't been able to bank the feeling. In the end, he'd been forced to work around it.

"He's going to make it," he assured her. "We got them all." He heard George sigh with relief.

"I'll leave you two alone," George said as he began to withdraw.

"What about his legs?" She wanted to know. "Are they affected?"

"We'll have to wait and see what happens once the swelling on his spinal cord goes down, but there's every indication that he'll be able to walk."

Thank you, God. Every deal I made, I'm good for it. "And the tumors?"

"There were five, not four," he told her. One had hidden behind another, giving the false reading. "Initial pathology says they're benign. But we have to do further testing."

* * *

Raven heard what she wanted to.

Benign.

And Blue would walk. He wouldn't spend the rest of his life in a wheelchair. Blue was going to be fine.

Relief shot through every part of her, drenching her, weakening her so that she thought her legs would cave under her.

With something that sounded very much like a whoop of joy, she threw her arms around Peter and kissed him. Kissed him long and hard with feeling that came from within the depths of her very soul. The anxiety that had been building within her these past six hours leeched out, leaving in its place an overwhelming energy that had absolutely no place to go.

Except to her lips.

To his surprise, Peter laced his arms around her and didn't just allow Raven to kiss him, but kissed her back. The surgery had taken a great deal out of him, as well, and now that it was over, now that he'd successfully removed the five tumors that had attached themselves to the boy's spinal column, he felt nothing but a breath-stealing relief.

Kissing her did nothing to restore his breath or his brain function. But it certainly made the rest of his body feel good.

Chapter Eight

Peter could feel things waking up within him, things that had been declared legally dead two years ago. Things he was stone-cold certain he would never feel again. But then Raven had kissed him the other night.

And here he was now, experiencing the sensation of capturing lightning in a bottle. He was the bottle, she was the lightning.

And there was even more feeling this time than the last. When she'd kissed him before, he'd felt a warmth, a compassion radiating from her. This time, he felt passion vibrating between them. Passion and a surge of something that hadn't been there before. It very nearly swept him off his feet.

He had no idea that he was capable of reacting at all, much less like this. The realization that he wanted her, really wanted her, burst upon his consciousness. Scaring the hell out of him.

Pulling back, he looked down at Raven, more shaken than he wanted to admit to. "You've got to stop doing that."

"Okay." The answer was issued on a breathless wave. He didn't believe her for a second.

"Am I interrupting something?"

Peter didn't have to turn around to know who the deep, gravelly voice belonged to. He'd heard it often enough in the last ten years. Fighting hard to reorient himself to his surroundings and to pick his brain up out of the pile of mush it had fallen into, he was surprised to find his one-time teacher and mentor standing behind them in the corridor.

Dr. Harry Welles was now the chief of surgery at Blair Memorial. Originally, the man had offered him a position once he'd finished with his residency at Aurora General upstate. He could think of nothing better than to work for and with a man he respected more than anyone else in the field of medicine. After Lisa and Becky's deaths, he had come completely unglued. Withdrawing into himself, he didn't leave his house, didn't go out at all. It was Welles who had dug him out of that all-consuming rubble of despair.

Two weeks after his self-imposed exile from life,

Welles had come to his house. He'd all but broken the door down. The man had arrived bringing not kind words but a kick in the rear to make him come around. As he'd stared at the surgeon blankly, Welles had informed him heatedly that he had a gift and that to waste it, to cheat others of it, would be not only a crime, but a sin. He had an obligation to the rest of humanity to make use of that gift. Pouring hot coffee and hotter words into him, Welles had made him come around.

Peter looked at the man now. Prematurely gray, Welles lived and breathed Blair Memorial. Not a surgery was scheduled or performed without his knowledge and his inherent interest.

"No," Peter muttered, stepping back from Raven. "You're not interrupting anything."

Welles's brown eyes took in Raven before fixing themselves back on his protégé. It was obvious that he thought otherwise, but would refrain from saying so. "How did it go?"

Peter blinked. Was Welles asking him about kissing Raven? "Excuse me?"

Welles's small mouth curved just a hint as amusement glinted in his eyes. "The surgery. On the Songbird boy," he qualified, enunciating each word slowly, like someone talking to a person who had just woken up from a long sleep. "How did it go?"

"We got the tumors," Peter informed him, struggling to regain his matter-of-fact manner. Kissing Raven and then being caught by the chief of surgery had addled his brain just a little. It took him a moment to recover.

Nodding, Welles looked genuinely pleased as he glanced toward Raven. "All four?"

Raven listened to the interest in man's voice. She was right, she thought, in coming here.

"Five," Peter corrected. "One tumor was hiding behind the others. We missed it in the CAT scan."

"Happens. Not that often, but it happens. Glad you're on your toes," Welles commended. He raised one somewhat shaggy eyebrow. "Benign?"

Peter stole a glance toward Raven. She was holding her breath. Did she expect him to say something different to his superior than he had to her? "First reading says they are."

"Excellent," Welles said with feeling. "Keep me posted." He clasped his hands behind his back like a fabled professor from another century rather than a man whose fingers were still known to perform magic in the operating room. "Carry on," he instructed as he began to walk away. This time the smile on his lips was even broader.

Raven moved a little closer to Peter so her voice wouldn't need to carry. "Who was that?"

He was acutely aware of her proximity. "Dr. Harry Welles. He's the chief of surgery here, has been for almost ten years." He watched the man round a corner and then disappear. ''Brilliant surgeon.''

There was almost awe in his voice, Raven thought. ''So are you.'' She said so without fanfare, as if the fact was one of life's givens. She pressed her lips together and looked up at him. The tears had returned, more urgent this time. She didn't bother trying to hold them back. ''I can't tell you how grateful I am to you.''

Peter's shrug was dismissive. ''I was just doing my job.''

''Not a job, a miracle.'' He heard the hitch in her voice and glanced at her. She covered her mouth with her hands, trying to compose herself at least a little. ''When you didn't come out...when the surgery just kept going on and on...I thought...I thought...'' She couldn't finish.

Oh, God, she was crying, he thought helplessly. He didn't know what to do with tears. He never had. A strong inclination to just walk away came over him, but he knew he couldn't do that. Somehow, he had to make her stop. ''Don't cry,'' he told her, his voice harsh with his own frustration and ineptitude. ''The surgery's over. He's still alive.''

''I know, that's why I'm crying.'' She saw the confusion come over his face. ''Because it is over. Because he's all right.'' Peter still didn't look as if he understood. ''These are tears of joy.''

''Oh. Maybe they should come labeled,'' he muttered. ''In my line of work, I usually see the other kind.''

A tear trickled down her cheek and she wiped it away with the back of her hand. Opening the small purse she kept with her, she began to rummage around for a handkerchief. ''Doesn't anyone ever cry when they thank you?''

''No one's ever thanked me.''

Unable to find a handkerchief, Raven used the heel of her hand to wipe away the tear stains on her cheeks. ''I can't believe that. What kind of people have you been dealing with?''

He made it a point to interact with patients and their families as little as humanly possible. Which was what made this whole scenario so unusual for him. Ordinarily, he would have allowed the doctor assisting him to give Raven the prognosis. For reasons he didn't quite understand, he'd left the operating room in search of her before he had even shed his surgical scrubs. He hadn't wanted her to suffer a single extra moment of crippling doubt.

But he wasn't about to explain himself or to let her know that this was an aberration. ''Because I usually let the assistant surgeon talk to the family.''

''If the surgery goes badly, you tell the patient's family. But if it goes well, you have someone else tell them?''

''Yes.''

''Why?'' She wanted to understand his reasons.

She wanted to understand him. "Don't you want to know how happy you made someone?"

She kept insisting on making it personal. He'd always been determined to keep it just the opposite. Breaking his rule this time had been a mistake. "It's not my job to make people happy. It's my job to use the latest technology and whatever skills I might possess to do what I said I would do."

Raven shook her head. The man put new meaning to the term self-efface.

"You make it sound as if you're some kind of mechanic doing a tune-up." He didn't try to negate the impression.

"Don't you realize how gifted you are? How special you are? How—"

Peter held his hand up. "Enough—"

To his surprise, she didn't back away, didn't just shoot a smile in his direction and pick another topic. She continued doggedly on. "No, I don't think it is. Peter, you've just done something wonderful. You've given my brother his childhood back. Why can't you congratulate yourself for that?"

He'd given Blue his childhood back, but he hadn't been able to give his wife and daughter their lives back. By the time he'd realized that it was *his* car that he'd seen all mangled up and had doubled back to the scene of the accident, Lisa and Becky were both gone. And all his skills couldn't bring them back.

He didn't answer her. Instead, he nodded toward the operating room. "Your brother's going to be in the recovery room for a couple of hours before they take him to the ICU—"

"ICU?" The initials sent a cold chill down her spine. Didn't people with intense problems stay there? Was there something he wasn't telling her, something that *was* wrong with Blue?

He saw the fear scurrying into her eyes. "Don't look so alarmed," he told her. "It's standard procedure for this kind of surgery. ICU is where all the latest equipment is kept. We need to monitor him—"

She was three thoughts ahead of him. "So something can still go wrong?"

She looked as if she was about to gather another one of her full heads of steam and go charging off. Peter placed his hands on her arms, as if that could somehow calm her down enough to listen.

"Blue's young, he's strong, but the hospital doesn't want to take any chances. There's someone at the nurses' station watching the monitors at all times. There's even one that goes off if your brother tries to turn over onto his back."

Blue was going to hate that, she thought. She flashed Peter an apologetic smile as she nodded. "Okay. I guess I am pretty frazzled."

"That's one word for it." Overwrought might have been another, he added silently. The last thing he needed was an overwrought guardian getting in the way. "Look, why don't you go home?" But even as he said it, he knew she wouldn't. She was one of those noble people who stood vigil. It made no matter if the object of their concern knew it or not, they stayed. "They're not going to let you stay in ICU," he told her crisply. "Visitors are only allowed in the area for five minutes every hour. Otherwise," he felt bound to add, "you can get in the nurses's way."

She had no intentions of getting in anyone's way. She also had no intention of leaving Blue. What if he woke up and she wasn't there? She didn't want him being scared. "I'm small. I can stay off to the side."

Yes, she was small, he thought. Small enough to fit neatly against him without leaving a ripple—except in his gut.

"Size doesn't matter. They have their rules," he informed her. Looking down, he realized that except for the surgical apron he'd shed, he was still wearing the clothes he'd operated in. "If you'll excuse me, I have to go change."

Raven pressed her lips together, stepping out of his way.

"I didn't mean to keep you," she told him, then added, "Thank you," with such heartfelt emotion that he thought she was going to cry again.

He hurried away before she did.

* * *

When he came down to the Intensive Care Unit later that evening to see how Blue was doing, the first person he saw was Raven. She sat on a chair beside her brother's bed, her feet tucked up beneath her, the ends of her colorful blouse hanging down halfway to the floor. One hand was lost to his view, the other was firmly holding Blue's, despite the fact that the boy was asleep. His small body was suspended a couple of inches above the mattress, lying in what looked like an oversize sling. It amazed him that the unnatural position didn't have the boy fully awake and complaining.

As if pretending that he hadn't seen her sitting there, Peter checked the chart at the foot of Blue's bed. Flipping the metal cover open, he saw that the boy had woken up from the anesthetic but, still very groggy, had fallen asleep again almost immediately.

Good, he thought, best thing in the world for him is sleep.

Glancing farther down the page, Peter saw that nothing eventful was happening—unless he counted the way seeing Raven affected him.

But that belonged on a different chart altogether.

Flipping the lid closed, he placed the chart back on the hook. Only then did he look at Raven. "What are you doing here?"

"Holding Blue's hand so he doesn't get frightened when he wakes up.'' To prove her point, she held up their interlocking fingers.

He moved closer to the chair. And to her. ''I thought I told you to go home.''

''You did.'' Her eyes bright, she made no apologies this time. ''I didn't.''

''I noticed.''

He looked disapprovingly at the chair. Her shoes were tucked in beneath it. One bare toe peeked out from beneath the yards of fabric. It raised thoughts about bare legs and bare bodies that he felt unequal to at the moment.

''How did you get them to let you drag a chair in here?'' And then he fed himself his own answer. There could be only one explanation. George. The man was shameless in his pandering, he thought. ''Did George—''

Raven shook her head. ''Last time I saw Mr. Grissom was outside the operating room. Sonia felt sorry for me.''

The name didn't mean anything to him right off the bat. ''Sonia?''

''Sonia Jakov. The head nurse at the desk,'' she added when there was no sign of recognition on his part.

As soon as she mentioned the woman's title, he knew who she was talking about. It also made her victory that much more incredible.

Peter glanced over to where the woman, known

as the Dragon Lady to the nurses who worked under her command, was sitting. And then a bit of color around her throat caught his eye. The last time he'd checked, multicolored scarves were not part of the required uniform. Sonia was wearing one of Raven's scarves.

"Did you bribe the head nurse?" he asked to know.

"It wasn't a bribe," she replied patiently. "Sonia asked me if I was related to the Songbird family. I told her that my brother and I were all that was left of the Songbird family. We talked for a little while. Did you know she has eleven brothers and sisters?"

Peter failed to see her point. "Why would I know that?"

She started to tell him, but then changed her mind. For now, she let it drop. He'd just saved her brother and didn't need any speeches. "Never mind. Anyway, when she told me she always loved the scarves my mother created, I gave her one."

He saw her purse sitting beneath her chair. It certainly didn't look very large. "Just how many scarves do you carry around with you?"

"Just enough," she answered. She couldn't help the self-satisfied expression that rose to her face. "She let me stay after that."

"Yes, small wonder." Peter frowned, looking at the chair again. It was one of those hard orange plastic ones that populated hospitals from one end of the country to the other. ''You planning to spend the night on that?''

She pretend to regard it. ''I've slept on harder surfaces.'' His concern, however gruffly voiced, made her smile. ''My parents led a pretty nomadic life when I was a kid.''

So had he in the early years. His father had been stationed in various parts of the country. He'd hated the moves, hated having to adjust to being the ''new kid'' again and again.

''What about school?''

She laughed softly at the memory. ''I must have attended fifteen different schools at one point or another.''

''Didn't you hate that?'' He wanted to know.

''No, I always liked meeting new people, finding new friends.''

Finding new friends. As if it was some kind of glorious treasure hunt. There was no doubt about it, he thought. They were worlds apart. Faced with relatively the same situation, they reacted to it in a completely different fashion.

''Anyway,'' she was saying, ''the point is, I'll be fine. Don't worry about me.''

''I'm not. I'm worried about George when he finds out you're sleeping on a chair. Man his age and condition tends to get heart attacks more readily.''

This time, she saw right through him. ''If you're

trying to use guilt to get me to leave, I'm afraid you're going to have to do better than that.'' She'd met people like George Grissom before. The man was bent on culling her favor because he needed a handy, open pocket for his hospital. She didn't fault him, she just understood him. ''I have a feeling that if I asked, Mr. Grissom would probably try to transfer an intensive care facility into one of the tower suites upstairs for me.''

Peter sighed. ''You're probably not wrong.''

Out of the corner of his eye, he saw the head nurse approach, then stand like a silent sentry, waiting in case he had any instructions for this newest addition to the ICU.

''Nice colors,'' he commented, indicating the scarf around her neck.

He saw the older woman exchanging glances with Raven. The nurse raised her head up proudly. ''Yes, they are,'' she acknowledged.

He knew when he was outnumbered. Peter lifted the top layer of bandage from the small of Blue's back. The boy stirred, but didn't wake up. He had Blue on the maximum dosage of painkiller for his size. Sleep was the best medicine for him now.

''Everything looks good here.'' Peter covered the boy again, then, stepping away from the bed, he looked at Sonia. ''Page me if anything changes.''

''Yes, Doctor.''

With a nod toward Raven, Peter left without another word.

"He's a spooky one," Sonia commented. Raven merely smiled.

Peter visited to the ICU one more time that evening. Actually, it was closer to the middle of the night. Unable to sleep—so what else was new?—he'd returned to the hospital at around one-thirty and walked quietly into the closed-off area. There were partitioned cubicles along both sides of the wall. Two thirds of the beds were empty, giving the space an eerie appearance.

As he moved closer to Blue's cubicle, he could see that Raven was still there. Curled up in the chair, she was sound asleep.

She really could acclimate anywhere, he thought.

Someone had given her a blanket, but it had slipped off and had pooled onto the floor around the base of the chair. He stepped around it to get to the chart.

Angling it to the available light, Peter read the newest notations. The boy was being given regular doses of antibiotics. He'd woken up twice, then fallen asleep again. Nothing eventful.

Satisfied, Peter placed the chart back at the foot of the bed, then stooped to pick up the blanket. As carefully as he could, he draped it over Raven. Moving quietly, he left the area, completely unaware that when he'd placed the blanket on her, Raven had woken up.

She'd followed him with her eyes and smiled to herself as Peter tiptoed out. With a small, contented sigh, Raven went back to sleep.

Chapter Nine

The following morning, he heard Raven talk to her brother as he approached the ICU cubicle. It was his first stop as he began his rounds before going to his office. Soft, melodic, soothing, he could almost feel the words as they drifted through the air.

What was there about the woman that he found so mesmerizing? That spoke to something inside of him?

And then, as if sensing his presence, Raven turned to look at him over her shoulder. "Hi."

He muttered something in return, not quite sure what, feeling strangely tongue-tied.

How did she manage to look so fresh, as if she'd

slept in a huge, comfortable double bed instead of on a chair that might have easily been used for penance by some tenth-century Christian? At the very least, she should have looked exhausted, her hair tousled and her face pale. But she looked like a fresh flower. Beautiful even without a trace of makeup on her face.

He would have said it was some trick accomplished through the crafty use of mirrors, except that there weren't any in the area.

Her eyes gazed not through him but into him, stirring up all sorts of things inside. Making him wish he were witty or at least coherent.

And what the hell did that have to do with the price of tomatoes? he upbraided himself. He was here in only one capacity, as a neurosurgeon, not a man who was inexplicably entranced by a woman who seemed as if she belonged inside the pages of a fairy tale.

He crossed to the foot of Blue's hospital bed and picked up the chart. Aside from filling in the gap between last night and this morning, the chart gave him something to focus on.

Clearing his throat, he nodded at Blue. "What kind of a night did he have?"

"He slept most of the time, thanks to the pain medication." She'd spent a rather wakeful night herself, watching him. And each time Blue had woken up, she could see his struggle to not cry out from the pain. Sonia had come to administer the prescribed dosage that allowed him to mercifully slip back into unconsciousness.

Blue tried to twist his head so that he could see him. To Peter, the boy looked like Peter Pan, sailing over the skies of London, looking for a place to land.

Where had that come from? he wondered. He wasn't given to imaginative descriptions. His were based on fact, not flights of fantasy. He was going to have to get a grip on himself.

"I hurt, Dr. Sullivan." It wasn't a whine, but a stated fact.

Peter moved over to where the boy could see him without having to crane his neck. "It's going to be a while before that changes."

She wished he hadn't phrased it that way. Honesty was a quality she admired. Up to a point. Where it ran up against hope and much needed optimism, she felt that honesty should take a back seat.

"Think yourself past it, honey." She'd already said the words to Blue several times, but she repeated them as if she'd just thought to share her philosophy with him. The philosophy that had seen her through so much already in her young life. Whenever she couldn't endure the moment she was in, she thought herself beyond it, sometimes hours, sometimes days. Anything that would get her to a stable point.

"All this pain will be behind you before you know it," she told him.

"Promise?"

Peter could see that it never occurred to Blue to doubt her. The boy was still young, he thought, still ignorant of all the things that could go wrong in life, despite the best of promises.

"Promise." Raising her eyes, she looked toward Peter for backup.

Something old and hardened within him told him to resist the silent entreaty. Something just a little larger told him to go along. What did it cost, making the boy feel better?

"Right," he finally said. "Every day, it'll get better. With a little time and some physical therapy, you'll be back to doing all the things boys your age do."

Whatever that was.

It had been a hundred years since he'd been a boy. And even then, under the strict discipline of his father, he'd been old for his age, expected to pull an adult's load long before his time.

Flipping back the chart cover, Peter quickly reviewed the new entries. Blue was getting his medication on time.

"I'm kind of hungry," the boy murmured.

Peter closed the chart again, looking at Blue in mild surprise. In his experience, most people were nauseated after surgery, not hungry. He hung the chart back in place and returned to the headboard so Blue could see him.

"Right now, you're getting all the nutrition you need through this feeding tube." He indicated one of the IV drips attached to Blue's thin arm.

Blue looked at the tube critically. "I'd like the straw to be in my mouth, not in my arm."

He noted that the simple request almost broke Raven's heart. It was obvious that she hated seeing him like this, with tubes running into his arms and as pale as a sheet.

"Soon, honey, soon," she told him. And then, bracing herself, willing her lips to curve and doing her best to hide her fears from Blue, she added, "I just want to talk to the doctor for a minute." She disengaged her hand from his and then grinned at him. "Don't fly off anywhere, okay?"

Blue sighed. It was obvious that he thought that if he could at least fly, all this might be worth putting up with. He did his best to return her encouraging smile.

"Okay."

Peter looked at her quizzically. She'd been so adamant all along about Blue being part of everything, what was she going to ask him in private? Raven motioned him to the side. He followed in her wake, trying not to notice that she still seemed to have an arousing scent about her that lingered in her path.

Turning, she glanced over to watch the back of Blue's head. She wanted to be sure he couldn't hear her. Not until she'd had a chance to digest this first.

"Did you get the results back yet?" She took another breath before she added, "For the tumors?"

The lab had been his first stop. He'd gotten there as a sleepy-eyed technician was unlocking the door. The latter hadn't looked too happy about having to search for results first thing in the morning.

"All benign." He gave her the answer she'd been waiting for, praying for, with absolutely no fanfare, as if he was reciting a stock market reading. He saw the glint in her eyes and he sighed. "You're going to cry again, aren't you?"

Raven pressed her lips together and nodded. She struggled to keep her voice from cracking when she spoke. "Sorry, can't help it."

"Raven?" Blue called to her uncertainly. He twisted and winced, trying to see her.

She realized that he'd heard the tone of her voice. He probably thought the worst. She rushed back to his bed, mentally saying, *Thank you, thank you.*

"Oh, God, I wish I could hug you right now." She knew that the slightest attempt would only translate into a world of pain for the boy. Instead, she laced both her hands around one of his and gave it just the tiniest squeeze, converting the surge of joy she felt down to the minus ten power. "It's good news, Blue. Wonderful news." Bending, she pressed her lips lightly to the back of his head. ''Everything's going to be perfect. *You're* going to be perfect.''

Peter noticed that the boy was taking his sister's tears in stride. Turning his head slightly so that he could make general eye contact with him, Blue confided, ''She cries when she's happy.''

Peter laughed. ''So I've noticed.''

She was notably too happy to care that they were making fun of her. Leaning over the top of the bed, she fished a tissue out of the small box on one of the side tables. She dried her eyes. Fresh tears insisted on replacing the ones that had been spent. She wiped those away, too.

''Men don't understand these things,'' she told them both with a laugh.

''That's what she always says when she's being strange,'' Blue told him.

Peter couldn't shake the feeling that the boy was trying to bond with him. Obviously this need to connect with strangers ran in the family. The thing was, he could feel himself being drawn in ever so slightly, as if he was part of some greater whole that they were part of as well.

''Don't give away all our family secrets at once,'' she cautioned her brother with a wink.

Peter shifted, but didn't move. He had other patients to see, more rounds to make. Why he hesitated didn't make any sense to him.

Neither did the fact that his shoes felt as if they'd been glued to the floor.

"I'll see you tonight," he told Blue.

The boy sighed staring at the wall. "I'll be here."

As he began to leave the ICU, Raven followed him to the entrance.

"Something else?" he asked, thinking that she'd undoubtedly come up with another question for him to wrestle with.

"I just wanted to thank you."

He thought of the way she'd kissed him outside the operating room. The way she'd managed to unseal his tight control. "You already did."

"No, I meant for putting the blanket back on me."

"You were awake for that?"

The smile she gave him could have melted the *Titantic*'s iceberg without leaving a hint of its existence.

"As you pointed out, that wasn't the most comfortable surface. I'd only dozed off for tiny snatches at a time. Thank you," she repeated.

"Yeah. Don't mention it." He inched toward the double doors that automatically sprang open when he was close enough. "Really," he added.

She watched him go through the doors and then have them yawn shut again. The man had a problem accepting gratitude, she thought. He was swiftly becoming her project of the month.

* * *

''Nurse, where's the boy in bed six?'' Peter asked when he returned that evening to the ICU. Preparing himself for another encounter with Raven, he'd found himself staring at an empty cubicle. The bed and the machines were gone.

Sonia looked up from the circular desk where she watched all the monitors for any signs of change. ''You mean, the Songbird boy? Mr. Grissom had him moved to one of the tower suites.''

''Would have been nice to have been told,'' Peter growled.

''Must have slipped everyone's mind,'' she murmured, getting back to her post.

Keeping his response to himself, Peter crossed to the bank of elevators that were programmed to take him straight to the top floor where the tower suites were located.

He had figured as much. Given half a chance, George Grissom would find a way to transfer the boy and everything he needed up to the tower suites. It was where all the VIPs who came to Blair stayed, no matter what the reason.

Better suited to a grand hotel, the suites were the last word in luxury, erasing every hint that the patient was staying in a hospital. He had no idea what being in one of the rooms cost, but he had a feeling that the people who occupied one of the suites didn't worry about such trivial things.

He was feeling unusually edgy tonight and the sensation grew with each step he took toward Blue's room. Peter caught hold of himself just before he knocked on the door and entered the vast room. It was like entering a florist's shop, or a nursery. There were flowers everywhere, with teddy bears and stuffed animals pock-marking several surfaces.

Blue still lay on his stomach, his middle suspended a couple of inches from his bed while his feet and head just barely made contact with the mattress. But unlike in the ICU, here his bed was turned around so that he could see his visitors. A large television was positioned so that he was able to watch its reflection in the full-length mirror that ran along the opposite wall.

"All the comforts of home, huh?" Peter noted as he walked in.

Raven's smile was immediate and warm when she saw him. And no amount of sealing himself off rendered him immune to it.

"If he was a trapeze artist," Raven quipped.

She'd changed her clothes, he noticed. Instead of the mass of swirling colors she'd had on earlier, she was wearing something soft and blue that brought out the intensity of her eyes.

As if she needed that, he thought. "You went home," he observed.

She looked down as if to remind herself what she

had on. "No, actually the clothes came to me. I had Connie bring them when she came to visit Blue. I haven't been out of the hospital since yesterday." She glanced toward the private bath. Instead of just the regulation handicap toilet, it was also equipped with a shower. "I did make use of the shower, though."

He nodded. "No extra charge."

An appreciative smile bloomed on her lips and she looked pleased. Why? he wondered. What had he said?

"You have a sense of humor." The fact took her completely by surprise.

He didn't think he'd ever been accused of that. "Not so anyone would notice."

"I did," she pointed out.

There it was again, that feeling that she was looking into him, into his thoughts, his soul. He knew it was absurd, but he couldn't shake the feeling.

"We've already established that you march to a different drummer." Trying to distance himself from his reaction to her, Peter looked back at the reason he was here. "How are his spirits?" It was a question he'd never heard himself asking before. Spirits or lack thereof weren't his realm. He dealt in what he could see, touch, taste, not assume. But somehow, the question seemed to be relevant here.

"Pretty good. The nurse and I already took him on a tiny stroll around his room."

Hearing them discuss his maiden run, Blue interjected, ''Tomorrow the hall.''

It was what she'd told Blue as he was placed, exhausted, back in the sling. It had quickly become his goal.

''He's amazingly resilient,'' she told Peter, affection emanating from every syllable. As Peter did a quick exam of the surgical site, she forced herself to watch despite the fact that the sight of blood made her stomach flip over. She was relieved when he moved the bandages back into place. ''Some of his friends came by earlier with their mothers.'' She exchanged grins with her brother. ''He's now officially the coolest kid in his group.''

A program came on that Blue was particularly fond of and Raven took the opportunity to move away from the bed for a moment. She lowered her voice as she said, ''He's pretending that his back doesn't hurt, but I know it does. He's always been a very brave little trouper. When do you think he can go home?''

She stood close to him again. So close that he could smell the soap she'd used. Something floral. Life up here in the tower suites was a world apart from the seven other floors below.

''Four days should do it,'' he told her. ''Ordinarily, the hospital likes as fast a turnaround as is medically feasible, but in this case I think George'll arrange a few extra days if you feel more comfortable with that.''

''What I'd be more comfortable with is taking Blue home as quickly as possible. If you said the word, he'd be out of the door like a shot, a slow-motion shot,'' she qualified, ''but a shot nonetheless.''

In the true nature of a child, Blue was already healing faster than an adult in his place. ''We'll take it one day at a time,'' Peter responded.

Raven looked at him for a long moment, her eyes holding his. ''That's all that anyone can ask.''

He had the strangest feeling that she wasn't talking about the same thing he was.

As he began to drive home after more than a full day at the hospital, he remembered that it had been some time since he'd even picked up a phone to call Renee. Taking out his cell phone, he placed an order for pizza at a local restaurant that wasn't far from her house.

He picked it up on his way. The aroma filled his car before he even got out of the parking lot, managing to block the scent that still lingered around him. Her scent.

''Hi, stranger.'' Renee's greeting was warm as she opened the door to him. ''Bearing gifts again? Or is this your subtle way of telling me you don't like my cooking?''

''I thought you could use a break—and I haven't had a pizza since I can't remember when.''

''You also can't remember to wear your coat,'' she chided, closing the door. ''Pete, it's cold out there.''

He saw she was wearing the scarf he'd dropped off the day after he'd received it. ''Not if you're wearing a scarf.''

She fingered it, smiling as she led the way to the kitchen. ''Lovely, isn't it?''

''On you,'' he allowed.

She opened the cupboard and took out two plates. ''You are good for me, Pete.'' Placing the plates on the table, she took two sodas from the refrigerator, then made herself as comfortable at the table as her condition allowed. ''So, how's your patient coming along?'' She fingered the scarf again to indicate who she was talking about.

Opening the pizza box, he took out a slice for his mother-in-law and then put one on his own plate. ''Surgery was uneventful.''

She laughed shortly at his modesty. ''Which is neurosurgeon shorthand for only one miracle was called for instead of three.''

He was doing his best to distance himself from the event as well as the boy and his sister. So far, he was having only marginal luck. Especially with Raven.

''He's mending fast. I discharged him at the end

of last week and he's due for his follow-up visit at the end of this week.'' It seemed that every time he looked at his calendar, that was the only appointment he saw. A hell of a thing for a man who liked to keep his surgical patients at arm's length.

Renee popped the top of her soda can. ''And then?''

He followed suit, taking a long drink. ''And then what?''

Renee grinned at him as she took a bite of her slice. ''I asked first.''

''I don't think I understand.''

''Yes, you do, you just want to play dumb, that's all.'' Renee shook her head. ''Doesn't become you, Peter.'' Playing along, Renee spelled it out for him. ''Are you going to see the boy after that?''

He'd already made his mind up about that. He'd talked to a neurologist earlier in the day. ''Dr. Rhys can take over.''

Her expression was patient. Understanding. He balked slightly at it.

''Maybe he won't be comfortable with Dr. Rhys,'' she suggested.

He could see the same argument coming from Raven once he told her about the change. So far, he'd held off, telling himself it was because the opportunity hadn't arisen yet.

''I'm a surgeon, Renee. That means I do surgeries. I make sure they take and then I move on.''

She looked at him knowingly. ''Seems to me that this one is a little different than the others.''

''Why?''

''For one thing,'' she pointed out blithely, ''you've never talked about any of the others. For another, his sister is very generous. I heard she's donating money for new equipment.''

Renee was an endless source of surprise to him. ''How did you find out about that?''

Taking another slice, she slipped it onto her plate. ''Unlike you, my doctor doesn't need much encouragement to talk.'' She became more animated. ''Seems that the hospital is very excited about this.''

''Free is always good.'' Uncomfortable with the direction the conversation was heading, he turned it back to her. ''So, how have you been feeling?''

She lifted only one shoulder, and marginally at that, in a half shrug.

''Can't complain.'' And then she paused, a self-depreciating smile curving her mouth. ''Well, I could, but what good would it do? Doesn't change anything.'' Her eyes met his. ''I've got good days and bad—just like you, Pete.'' Leaning over the table, in typical motherly fashion she pushed back the hair that was falling into his eyes. Her voice was soft as she said, ''She would have wanted you to be happy, you know.''

''Who?''

"Lisa. She wouldn't have wanted you to spend your whole life mourning her."

His appetite waning, he put the second slice down and looked at the woman across from him. "It's not something I can control."

"Sure you can. Mind over matter, Pete." Her tone was firm, encouraging. "You of all people know that."

He picked up on the words she'd used and fed them back to her. "In my mind, ever since Lisa's been gone, nothing else seems to matter."

"It should," she insisted. And then, because she must have known how Peter reacted when too much pressure was applied, she backed off. "Now then, did you tell her how much I liked the scarf?"

He hadn't said anything to Raven about the gift she'd given him for his mother-in-law. "Slipped my mind."

She passed a napkin to him. "Then you'll have something to talk about the next time you see her."

Accepting it, he wiped his fingers before picking up the soda can again. "The next time I see her will be for her brother's follow-up."

Renee nodded, reading between the lines. "I think you should do a follow-up of your own after that."

He sighed. He knew she meant well, but at the end of a long day, it was hard to hang on to his temper. "You don't stop, do you?"

Renee just smiled back at him. "Not until I reach my goal."

"Which is?"

"Seeing you happy," she answered simply, then added, "And maybe getting a grandchild out of the bargain."

"Just how do you figure that?"

Renee laughed. "At your age and position, I'd think you'd have a pretty good handle on the birds and bees by now, but if you want—"

He cut her off. "You know what I mean."

The amusement faded. Renee grew serious. "You're my son-in-law, Pete, and you've become like a son to me. Nothing is going to change that. When a son has a child, that automatically makes his mother a grandmother."

"Overlooking a few things here, aren't we?"

"Only way to go through life, Pete. Fix what you can, accept what you can't and always, always look for the upside of everything."

He suddenly felt very tired. "What was the upside of Lisa and Becky dying?"

Renee never hesitated for a moment. "That you weren't in the car with them." She placed her hand on top of his, making a connection. Willing him to take strength from it. "That I still have you."

He felt completely outnumbered as he shook his head. "You're a lot like her."

"Lisa?"

''No, Raven.''

Renee beamed at him as she reached for a third slice. ''I like her already.''

The problem was, he was beginning to think that perhaps he did, too.

Chapter Ten

Putting aside his stethoscope, Peter motioned for Blue to get dressed again. With the help of his sister, the boy got dressed then followed him into the next room, which was his office. Blue sat in the chair that faced his desk. Raven took the other chair.

Both of them waited for him to say something.

"He's made remarkable progress in an incredible amount of time."

As a rule, he wasn't given to using glowing adjectives. But after examining the boy and looking at the latest set of scans that had been taken, he found that there was no other way to describe the situation. If an adult had had the kind of operation that Blue had gone through, it would have taken at least ten days before they would have attempted so many assisted steps from their bed. That would be followed by a period of time in which they would have to rely on a walker. Blue broke the rules.

With the aid of a nurse and his sister, Blue had been down the hall a day and a half after his surgery and had come in for his two-week follow-up holding on to Raven's arm. Otherwise, he had entered unassisted.

Peter thought of what Raven had endured emotionally after her parents had been killed. Obviously courage or grit ran in the family.

He leaned back in his chair, momentarily giving in to himself. He studied not the boy but Raven. Suppressing a sigh, he knew he had to make a break and soon. The first step was to discharge Blue from his care, because that was his way, and because he'd been looking forward to the appointment too much.

Looking forward to seeing Raven.

That was the truth of it, no matter how deeply he tried to bury the fact. She'd been lingering on his mind too much.

He was getting too close to her.

He didn't want to get close to anyone, not after what he'd already gone through. Having his heart sliced up into tiny slivers once in a lifetime was more than enough for him.

* * *

Raven could always sense when something was wrong. But this time she knew it didn't have anything to do with Blue, but with the darkly handsome man who was looking at them so solemnly.

Turning, she smiled at her brother. "He's always been resilient that way," she said fondly. "So, when do you want to see him again?"

"I don't." The words were crisp, without feeling. Final.

So that was why he looked the way he did, Raven thought.

He was cutting them loose. Something inside her chest stung, surprising her at the depth of the impact. "I thought this kind of surgery required several follow-ups. I know I said Blue was resilient, but—"

"I'm handing the case off to Dr. William Rhys. He's a board certified neurologist, on staff here at Blair and he can follow your brother's progress from here on in."

"I see." Raven felt as if something had hit her in the hollow of her stomach. It wasn't quite like when she'd been told about her parents' car accident, but it was close enough to numb her for a moment.

It was Blue who broke the silence, allowing her to gather herself together. "Don't you want to see me again, Dr. Sullivan?"

This was something new. He'd never been put on

the spot by a patient before. But then, he'd never spent this much time with a surgical patient before, either. Served him right for getting this involved. For allowing a face, a voice, to become imbedded in his mind along with all the necessary statistics and procedures that were needed to successfully perform the operation in the first place.

Peter tried his best to sound detached, not understanding why it seemed so much harder than usual for him to do it this time around.

''Dr. Rhys is more qualified for follow-up care than I am,'' he told Blue.

Blue looked at him, his open face completely mystified. ''Why? You did it. If something's wrong, wouldn't you know better than anyone?''

Unable to help himself, Peter looked at Raven, surprised by the simple depth of the boy's question. ''Are you sure he's only seven?''

Her mouth curved. He could almost feel it curving against his mouth. It convinced him that he'd made the right choice. If he waited even a little while, it might be too late for him.

''Seven going on forty,'' Raven replied. ''But Blue has a point, you know, Peter. More than anyone else, you are the one who's the most familiar with the case. Someone else would have to get up to speed before they could do Blue any good.''

''Dr. Rhys is familiar with cases like your brother's.'' He didn't like her challenging his decision—especially when a very small part of him felt as if he was taking the coward's way out. "This is the way I've always handled my cases."

She looked at him knowingly. "So it's just sew and go, is that it?"

He pulled himself up in his chair. He'd never had to defend himself before. "I'm a surgeon, Raven. By definition, that means I operate."

She just wasn't buying his quick dismissal of responsibility. "You're not some two-dimensional noun in an oversize dictionary, Peter. You're allowed to expand." She leaned forward on her chair. "We don't bite. Honest."

He didn't know about that. He felt as if he'd been bitten and if he didn't act quickly, there was no telling how fast the serum would spread within his system. Or just what it would do, what it would undermine once it did spread. Without being completely conscious of the process, he'd allowed both Raven and her brother to get to him. It was time he pulled himself free.

Opening his desk, he took out one of William Rhys's business cards and held it out to Raven. "Here's Dr. Rhys's phone number. His nurse is already expecting your call."

Raven took the card after a beat, closing her hand around the small shell-colored paper. The look in her eyes told him that she knew this wasn't about standard procedure. That he'd felt a connection being made and that it scared him.

He wasn't the only one.

"Then I guess we shouldn't disappoint her." Raven rose to her feet. Taking his arm, she supported Blue as he got to his. "Thank you for everything, Doctor." She gave him one of her dazzling smiles, the kind someone had once told her could unfreeze the hardest heart. "And if you should ever feel like taking another look at your handiwork, feel free to stop by. You already know where we live."

Peter made no response. He merely nodded as he remained behind his desk. It was a safe place to be as he watched them leave the office.

Yes, he thought, he already knew where they lived, but it was a piece of information he was going to do his best to delete from his memory.

He couldn't delete it.

Worse, after a week, it seemed to be on his mind constantly. Along with the woman he didn't want to see. The more he attempted to ignore it, the more it loomed over him, like some huge billboard on the side of the road that only kept getting larger and larger.

He tried, in vain, to cram as much work as he could into a day, to keep at bay thoughts of Raven, of the way her body had leaned into his when she'd kissed him.

The thoughts came anyway, like relentless kamikaze soldiers with but one focus. To completely disrupt life as he knew it.

He held out as long as he could. It amounted to fifteen days.

On the fifteenth evening, he discovered himself driving toward the Songbird estate. His rounds had been completed and for once, there was neither someone nervously sitting in his office, waiting to discuss a possible surgery, nor a single scheduled surgery.

Two weeks had gone by.

Two weeks in which, except for today, his life had been as hectic as it got. Dr. Welles had approached him not two days ago, asking him for his opinion. It wasn't about some case he was overseeing, but about himself. Severe headaches had caused the chief of surgery to have CAT scans taken of his brain. The tests had revealed an aneurysm. Surgery was the only option he would consider. And Welles wanted him to perform the surgery.

Peter had agreed, but not without some silent concern. Despite this newest burden on his shoulders, he caught himself thinking about the woman whose smile refused to erase itself from his mind. The memory of her smile, her eyes and the feel of her mouth on his kept insisting on replaying itself over and over again.

Only when he was in the middle of surgery did these troublesome images disappear. But he had no idea how long it would be before they disrupted his work. So he decided to take the bull by the horns. It was a known fact that in many instances, memories were far better than the actual event, or the actual person involved. He was hoping that this applied to a raven-haired woman with laughing blue eyes.

Before he was aware of any time having gone by, Peter pulled up to her driveway. Highlighted by several strategically positioned old-fashioned streetlamps, the driveway appeared to be just as colorful at night as it had been when he'd seen it in broad daylight.

Peter was out of the car and ringing the front doorbell before he could talk himself out of it. But once he had pressed the bell and the door hadn't opened immediately, he came to his senses. This was crazy. What was he doing here? He needed to go home, not chase after…what? A dream? He knew what happened when you chased after dreams. Dreams ended. They always ended, leaving you with nothing.

Better not to have anything than to mourn its loss.

Turning on his heel, Peter began to walk away.

He heard the sound of a door opening behind

him. Heard Raven calling out his name in both surprise and pure delight.

"Peter?" Not waiting for him to respond or to turn around, Raven ran out of the house. In a few quick strides, she managed to get in front of him, aborting his exit. "Peter, you've got to give me a chance to get to the door." She laughed, her hand on his arm, holding him in place. "It's a big house."

Damn it, she looked better than he remembered.

For once, she wasn't dressed like some Gypsy or woodland sprite fresh out of the forest. She wore a simple pullover blouse that hugged her torso the way he found himself longing to. The jeans she had on were faded and adhered to her body like a second skin. He found himself jealous of frayed denim and convinced that he was losing his mind.

She appeared a great deal smaller now than she had in his office or the hospital. He realized that it was because she was barefoot. It had to be no more than thirty-five degrees outside and she stood on the pavers without shoes or socks. Raven pivoted on the balls of her bare feet, as if sustaining minimum contact with the cold ground could keep her from shivering.

Peter looked at her accusingly. "You're barefoot."

She ignored his tone. "I never wear shoes in the house unless there's a party going on," she told him as she hooked her bare arms through his and began to tug him back toward the door. "C'mon into the house before I catch something more than you," she teased.

He was behaving like an idiot, he upbraided himself again. There was no reason for him to be here. None except that he'd missed her. He looked over his shoulder toward his car. "I should really—"

She smiled up into his eyes. "Yes, you should really," she murmured. The next moment, as she crossed the threshold still holding on to her prize, she was calling out, "Blue, guess who's here?" Not waiting for a response, she answered the question for him. "Dr. Sullivan's decided to pay you a surprise check-up visit."

The house echoed with the melody of her voice, much like his head had for the past two weeks. Turning to face him, she gave him the feeling that she was not about to allow him to make a face-saving getaway.

"Why don't I take your coat and you can look in on your patient?" she suggested. "He's in the family room," she added. Moving behind him, Raven began to help him off with his overcoat.

He twisted around, trying to get a look at her. Trying to get her to stop. "I can do this myself."

She peeked around his shoulder, her expression impish. "I don't trust you. If I leave it up to you, you and your coat will bolt out of here. And after it took you two weeks to finally show up.'' With a yank, she successfully removed the camel-colored overcoat.

''You were expecting me?''

''Sure,'' she told him glibly. ''Didn't you know? I cast a spell on you. You were bound to show up sooner or later. I just thought it would be a little sooner.'' He looked as if he believed her. Unable to hold it back any longer, she laughed and shook her head. ''I am kidding, Peter. I'm not a Gypsy or a would-be witch. I don't dabble in black magic or white, or any other color for that matter.'' When she'd been a little girl, other kids would tease her because her mother was three-quarters Navajo and would sometimes create sand pictures the way her grandmother had taught her to do. ''But I was really hoping you'd come by to look in on him.'' After a second, because she was truthful, she added, ''And me.''

He didn't know about her not being a witch. Or about her not casting a spell on him. If he were being honest, he certainly felt bewitched.

Why else would he be here?

Why else would he be bending his own rules, especially after he'd successfully made the break and sent the boy to another doctor? He'd been in the clear. And yet, here he was, hiding behind his credentials, playing the concerned doctor when all he really wanted to do was to breathe in the scent of her hair one more time. See her smile one more time. Feel her vibrancy.

Feel her against him.

Damn, but he was losing it.

Blue had wiggled off the sofa in the family room and was at the threshold the moment he approached the room. The boy's face was a wreath of smiles, as if he was greeting a long lost friend instead of a physician he'd only seen a handful of times.

What kind of people were these? Peter wondered.

Bracing himself, he crossed the threshold and walked over to the boy. "So, how are you doing?"

"Great." With a display of boundless energy, Blue attached himself to Peter's other arm. "You like video games?"

"What?"

"Video games," Blue repeated patiently, looking up at him serenely. Peter saw the huge TV monitor with a game in progress, presently frozen. He suddenly felt very ignorant.

Raven indicated the screen. It featured the very latest in the video craze. "Don't you hear about video games in doctorville?" she asked, amusement shining in her eyes.

"I don't have time for games in 'doctorville,'" he informed her coolly.

"Everyone has time for games," Blue insisted. "It helps you relax. You could be any color you wanted," Blue offered.

"Thanks, but I'll pass." He needed to leave, before he gave in to the impulse to remain, Peter thought. Gave in to the need to be part of something that had been ripped away from him. This wasn't his family. Blue wasn't his child and this wasn't his wife. "I was in the neighborhood and decided to see how you were doing."

He saw amused disbelief in Raven's eyes, and he decided to ignore her.

"Great," Blue volunteered. "I'm doing great."

Raven held up one of the control panels that was attached to the console. "He might do better if you stuck around and played a game or two."

He'd never held one of those in his hands, didn't even know the first thing that was necessary to make it work. "I don't think so."

If Blue was disappointed, he hid it well. "Where do you want me?" he asked Peter.

"For what?"

Obviously thinking that he was being teased, Blue laughed. "For the exam, silly."

"Right here will be fine."

It was a quick exam, conducted by a doctor who only wanted to make a getaway before he made a complete idiot of himself. If it wasn't too late already. In short order Peter was packing up his instruments, placing them into the black bag Dr. Welles had presented to him when he'd graduated from medical school. "He's doing very well."

"Yes, I know." She was pleased beyond words that each day found Blue a little less pain encumbered than the last. "Maybe even better than you." She saw him look at her sharply and she offered him a smile in response. "Now can you play?"

Like a man struggling against being taken down by the undertow, he took a step back from her. His bag was in his hand.

"No, I've got to get going. Goodbye, Blue, Raven." He nodded at her.

She matched him retreating step for retreating step. She had her mother's affinity for recognizing souls in pain and Peter Sullivan was definitely a soul in pain. "Have you had dinner yet? I could whip up something in the kitchen—"

Fighting the temptation to give in, he cut her short. "No, thanks, I need to leave."

"If you say so." Need to escape is more like it, she thought.

Still barefoot, she followed him outside. The weather had dropped another few degrees. She wrapped her arms around herself as she stood looking at him.

"You don't have to go, you know."

"Yes, I do."

He had to leave, *now,* because he was having something very close to a panic attack, born of the desire to remain. To stay here and play some absurd video game and pretend that he was part of something, part of a unit, instead of the loner he was.

But it would be a lie.

He wasn't part of this family, wasn't part of anything at all really and he'd already made his peace with that before Raven had come on the scene and stirred things up inside of him. With a muttered good-night, he moved away quickly before the temptation to kiss her broke through his not-quite-steely reserve.

Peter got into his car and slammed the door shut. Putting his key into the ignition, he turned it and heard a whining noise before all sound suddenly died. He turned the key again and this time, there wasn't even the whining sound.

Nothing.

A third attempt brought the same results.

Raven walked up to the open window on the driver's side and looked in. "Problem?"

Even with a door between them, it felt as if she was too close. The breeze brought her scent right to him, filling the car. Filling his head.

"My car won't start."

He saw the grin spread slowly, taking in every single feature. "That would explain the pitiful noise."

He sighed. His hand on the door, he indicated that he wanted to get out. She took a step back, allowing him to exit. Taking out his cell phone,

Peter began to hit a series of buttons, only to be rewarded with an annoying beep.

"I think your battery's low," she volunteered, pressing her lips together to hold back another smile.

He looked at the message written across his screen. It confirmed what she'd just told him. And then the message and the last of the light faded from the screen, leaving it blank.

Peter bit back a choice word. He'd forgotten to charge his phone last night.

When it rained, it poured.

Disgusted, he shoved the useless phone back into his pocket. Just what he needed, a dead car and a dead phone. Banking down his anger, he looked at her. "Can I use your phone?"

"You want to call a cab?" she guessed.

He shook his head. "No, I need someone to take a look at this. I've got roadside service," he added in case she wondered who he was planning on calling at this time of the evening.

"Don't bother calling them yet," she told him. "Let me go back into the house and get a flashlight and some tools."

He saw no point in doing that. Automobiles fell under the realm of mystery as far as he was concerned. "I'm not handy with cars," he called after her.

She looked over her shoulder just before she disappeared into the house. "But I am."

Chapter Eleven

"Well, technically, the problem shouldn't be your battery," Raven told him several minutes later.

She'd returned carrying a toolbox that was a lot larger than he would have expected someone like her to have. Setting it down, she'd instructed him to pop the hood of his car. Then, as he'd watched, she'd turned on a flashlight to help her conduct a quick exam of the engine and its surrounding parts.

She glanced at him to see if he was listening. "That's less than a year old."

Peter stared at her. "How would you know something like that?"

Shining her flashlight along the battery cables,

Raven leaned in as she continued to check out the various connections. He tried not to notice how snug her jeans fit.

"Well, my mother was three-quarter Navajo and one of her grandfathers was a tribal medicine man who was said to have great psychic powers." She looked at him over her shoulder and grinned broadly. "That, and the month and year are scratched onto the top of the battery." Straightening, she brushed off one hand against her back pocket. It took effort on his part not to allow his mind to travel there. "They do that so you know when to replace it."

"Oh."

Peter stopped looking in under the hood. He had no idea what he was looking at anyway and he felt like an idiot. He was a man and he should have at least known about the date on the battery. It didn't exactly take any technical know-how.

Raven saw the look of self-disgust on his face. "Hey, we all have our specialties." Moving to the other side, she shone the flashlight on the distributor cap. There were no telltale marks on it, indicating a possible burn. She ruled it out as the source of the problem. "Yours is performing miracles in the operating room."

He crossed his arms in front of him as he studied her. "And what's yours?"

"I'm not sure yet," she answered cheerfully.

"I'm kind of a Jill of all trades, I guess. A little bit of everything, a whole lot of nothing." She shrugged her shoulders. Her hair brushed along the one closest to him. "Something like that."

There was no way that the last part of the description applied to her. She was as far from "a whole lot of nothing" as he was from being gregarious, and he had a feeling that she knew it.

Peter nodded toward his uncooperative vehicle. "Where did you learn to fix cars?"

"Tinker with cars," she corrected. She was a long way from being a mechanic, the way her father had been. The man had been a positive magician when it came to their temperamental mode of transportation. "My dad. Anastasia was always breaking down or having some kind of problem or other and he'd always find a way to eke yet another thousand miles out of her."

"Anastasia?" he echoed. She jumped around too much. Keeping up with her was a challenge.

"That's what we called the old 'bus.' Daisy for short." Her eyes teased his as she stopped to look at him. "Don't you name your car?"

"No."

"Maybe that's part of the problem. You should." The way she said it left no room for debate. "I think Daisy had close to four hundred thousand miles on her when she finally gave up the ghost. Dad didn't want to junk her after all the faithful service she'd give us, so he built Mom's first 'workshop' in it.''

Raven sounded as if she was talking about a beloved relative instead of a vehicle, he thought. She lived in a whole different world than he did. He had trouble finding human qualities in people, she found them in inanimate objects.

Peter focused on something he could understand. Or try to. ''Four hundred thousand miles? Just how much traveling did you do in that thing?''

She laughed. ''Not as much as you think. Dad got Daisy used. It was all he could afford.'' The smile he saw on her face was slightly distant, as if her thoughts were taking her years into the past. ''My parents were very happy in that old bus.''

And then, as if the memory had suddenly become too painful to deal with, she stopped and looked beneath the hood.

He moved in closer, again looking at he didn't know what. ''Figure out what's wrong?''

She nodded as a thoughtful expression slipped over her features. ''You know, someone once told me that if you hear hoofbeats, think horse, not zebra.''

He wasn't following. ''You talking about the car's horsepower, or is this your way of telling me to get a horse?''

''Neither.'' She laughed. The man was way too literal. He needed to lighten up. Her mother would have said he was just the kind of man who needed saving. And she was pretty confident that she was up to the job. "I'm talking about things are usually simpler than we think they are." She looked at him for a long moment before finally squatting to rummage through the toolbox she had left open at her feet.

Peter had the distinct feeling that this half Navajo princess, half wild Gypsy wasn't actually talking about the car trouble he was having. But she was wrong. Things weren't usually simpler, what they were was complicated. And, as he watched her, he felt they were growing more complicated by the moment.

"*Voilá.*" Popping up to her feet, she held what looked like a toothbrush with metal teeth in one hand and a box of baking soda in the other.

What little imagination he'd been granted at birth extended only to surgical procedures performed within antiseptic operating rooms. "Okay, I'm stumped, what are you going to do?"

"Not brush my teeth," she quipped, as if guessing what his one thought might be.

Taking the small bottle of water she'd brought out along with the toolbox, she poured some into an old plastic dish she'd dug out of the box. She added some of the baking soda and mixed the two together to form a liquid paste. Satisfied with the consistency, she undid the connectors that were over the battery terminals and cleaned first one, then the other with the paste she'd just made.

The whole process seemed strange to him, like a home remedy applied to sophisticated machinery. "What's that supposed to do?"

"Sometimes there's too much acid built up over the wires, making it hard to get a good connection. If you don't have a good connection, the battery won't start your engine. The baking soda gets rid of the gunk."

"Scientific word."

She flashed a smile that was dazzling even in the limited light.

"I rather like it." Finished, she reconnected the wires to the terminals, tightening each with a small wrench. She set aside the remainder of the mixture. "Okay, try it now."

Getting in behind the wheel, Peter skeptically inserted his key into the ignition and turned it. The engine came to life as if it had only been sleeping. He turned it off and tried it again with the same results. He was more than a little surprised. "You did it."

She flipped the toolbox closed with her bare foot. "Sure, black magic and white baking soda, works every time."

As the car idled, he looked at her. "What do I owe you?"

"Nothing."

"I don't like being in debt."

"Okay." Her eyes met his. "Time."

"Excuse me?"

"Time," Raven repeated. She flipped her hair over her shoulder, completely innocent of how seductive she was to him. "Pay me in time." She could see he still wasn't following her. "Come back into the house. Spend a little time with Blue and me. He'd love it." It went without saying that she welcomed it, as well.

He was an adult, Blue was seven. What could they have in common? "Why?"

"Because, if you haven't noticed by now, my little brother's taken a shine to you." Her smile grew broader. "I know he'd love to teach you how to play a video game. Might help you to unwind."

"I don't need to unwind." As if in direct contradiction, he stiffened somewhat.

"Only old-fashioned clocks don't need to unwind. Tension is good, it keeps us sharp and alert." Squatting, she flipped the dual locks on the toolbox, then picked it up. "But too much tension and we're liable to go off like a Roman candle." Abandoning the water bottle, she took hold of his arm with her free hand, silently letting him know that the debate was over.

It wasn't as if he had anything planned for the remainder of the evening. And he did hate being in anyone's debt. It was like having something hanging over him. With a sigh that was not completely resigned, he took the toolbox from her. ''I suppose a little while can't hurt.''

''Not a bit,'' she promised him.

As he walked back inside, he couldn't shake the feeling that she was wrong.

''I think you wore him out,'' she told Peter in a whisper that found its way straight into his gut, tightening it until he could hardly breathe.

Blue sat between them on the sofa, or rather, lay slumped between them on the sofa. Protesting that he wasn't the least bit tired, the boy had fallen asleep almost midword. The control pad was still clutched tightly in his hand.

Peter looked at the dizzying track exhibited on the television screen. Still in possession of his own control pad, he straightened out his vehicle, making it to the finish line.

He glanced toward Raven. ''Does that mean I finally won a race?''

''By default,'' she pointed out with a laugh he found incredibly sexy.

He tossed the control pad on the coffee table. ''Hey, a win's a win.''

She switched off the game. The noise level crashed. Suddenly all that was heard was the sound of Blue's even breathing.

''I like you this way.''

He wished she wouldn't look at him like that. "What way?"

"Relaxed." But even now, she thought, he was reverting back to his other persona. Guarded. Wary. As if he expected something to come crashing down all around him.

Peter felt as if she was seeing right through him and wanted to change the subject. "What do you want to do with him?"

"Well, I've tried auctioning him off," she laughed, "but no one's ever offered enough money for me to recoup what I've already invested in him, so I guess I'll just have to put him to bed and keep him."

For a second, when Raven started, he thought she was serious. And then he laughed, too, shaking his head. Careful not to disturb the boy, he rose to his feet, then picked Blue up. Her toolbox had felt heavier.

He looked at Raven in surprise. "He hardly weighs anything."

"Takes after my mother's side of the family. They were small people." Stepping away from the coffee table, she led the way out of the family room. She glanced over her shoulder. Something inside her constricted. He looked so right, holding Blue like that. "I'm hoping for a growth spurt for him, though. I had one when I was twelve."

"To become the giant you are now?" She was

willowy, but far from tall. He doubted that, in her bare feet, she was more than five-four. Maybe less.

"I was a peanut compared to this," she informed him. She smiled fondly at her sleeping brother. "Every inch counts when you're short."

In the foyer, Peter looked around. There was a whole lot of house no matter which way they went. When he'd asked her earlier, she'd told him casually that there were fifteen bedrooms in the house.

"Which way?"

She pointed him toward the staircase. "It's the first door to the left at the top of the stairs." Letting him go first, she followed Peter up.

What did someone do with fifteen bedrooms? he caught himself wondering. She could have housed three separate families here without blinking an eye. Was all this space just for her and her brother?

"I haven't seen anyone here all night beside the two of you."

"Connie took the day off to see some friends and we don't really have much household help. The cleaning crew comes once a week. The gardeners show up every two." Coming to the landing, she shrugged. "That's about it, really."

She knew what Peter was probably thinking, that this was too much house for two people, three if you counted Connie. But this was home, the first one she'd ever had that hadn't had wheels attached to it since she'd been a little girl on the farm. Her father had picked out this house for her mother and because of that, it was a special place to her. And also because of that, it would also always be home.

He waited for her to open the right door, then walked into the room. Done in beige and light blue, it looked like a child's idea of heaven. Blue had his own television set, four of the latest video systems not to mention countless games. It was a wonder the boy in his arms wasn't hopelessly spoiled, but everything about him indicated that he was a well-adjusted, mature-for-his-age boy. Peter figured that was a credit to the way his sister had raised him.

"No chauffeur?"

"I like the feel of the wheel in my hands."

The truth of it was, though she liked to think of herself as a free spirit, she also liked to be in control of things. Destiny had taken away two of the people she'd loved most in this world. She couldn't harness destiny, but she wanted to keep as much as she could reined in and within her control.

She nodded toward the king-size bed. "Just put him right there." When he did, she crossed to the bed. There was no need to take off his shoes since Blue was barefoot like she was. Taking the edge of the comforter, she folded it over and covered him with it.

Peter looked on, puzzled. When he was a child, there had been an entire ritual to follow before going to bed. His father had made sure of it. If he skipped brushing his teeth or laying out his clothes for the next day, there were repercussions to face. Going to bed in his clothes—the way all little boys fantasized about at one time or another—had earned him a slap across the face.

"Aren't you going to undress him?"

She shook her head. "It might wake him." Raven paused to switch the lamp to its lowest setting. "He's slept in his clothes before."

"What about the light?" He nodded at the lamp. "Aren't you going to close it?"

Raven crossed the threshold out into the hall. "Blue's afraid of the dark. I don't see the point in traumatizing him by insisting on having the light off. He'll grow out of it. My parents were very understanding. I was fifteen before I slept with the light off. It didn't hurt me any."

"God, but you are unorthodox."

But even as he said it, there was a note of admiration in his voice. Blue was so well adjusted because he had someone like Raven in his life. Someone who didn't just live by rules and regulations, but who knew how and when to bend.

She eased the door closed behind her. Her mouth quirked in a smile. "Why? Because I scrub battery terminals with baking soda and let my kid brother sleep in his clothes with the light on?"

"That," he allowed, "and a whole bunch of other things, as well."

He combed his fingers through her hair, loving the feel of it. It was as if his hands had taken on a life of their own, operating independently of him. The rest of his body wanted desperately to follow suit, leaving his mind, his iron will, in the dust.

Exhaling slowly, Raven rocked forward slightly on her toes. Her eyes never left his. "Such as?"

He felt like a man hypnotized. Her mouth was inches away from his. All he had to do was to bend his head. All he had to do was to give in to the almost fierce demands that hammered away at him.

All.

It was a huge word. A huge step.

Like someone about to drown in the rapids, he struggled to survive, to reach the bank. "Raven, if you don't move back, I'm going to kiss you."

She stayed exactly where she was, rising up just a little higher, a little closer. "Would that be so very bad?"

Damn but he wanted her. Wanted what he couldn't, what he shouldn't, have. "It might be. For me."

He watched as the smile slowly rolled over her features, capturing them the way the early morning sun captured the sleeping terrain as it spread its rays over the land. "Why don't you try it and see what happens?"

He knew what was going to happen.

Knew before he covered her mouth with his.

Knew, probably, the moment he had agreed to come back into the house with her after she'd revived his car.

He was going to make love with her.

If he meant to resist the thought, he found that he hadn't the strength. He wanted this too much. Peter folded his arms around her as the kiss deepened almost of its own accord, taking him prisoner as it did so.

She made his head spin, his blood surge. She made him remember just how long it had been since he'd wanted a woman this badly.

Two years.

An eternity ago.

If there was guilt, he blocked it, needing just this once to have this wild, unorthodox woman who made him forget everything else. To give in to the passion and make love with her. To remember what he'd tried so hard to bury—that he was a man, with a man's desires, a man's feelings. Because this was the only time he could allow himself to have feelings. When he made love.

And if it was wrong—and he knew in his heart that it had to be—then he would deal with it all tomorrow. But not now.

This was what she'd wanted, what she'd waited for. What she'd known was on the verge of happening. She'd teased him about there being psychic abilities in her family, but in truth, there had been some. Her great-grandfather had been a seer, as well, and there were times she just knew things were going to happen. Just before she'd accepted her diploma, she'd looked at three empty seats in the audience, seats that her family might have been in, and known with a chilling certainty that something had happened to them even before anyone had come to tell her. And when she'd met Peter that very first time in the hospital, even though she hadn't been sure if he was the one to operate on Blue, she'd sensed that one day they would be together like this.

''My room is just down the hall,'' she breathed against his mouth when her brain allowed her to string a few words together.

She could sense that he was trying very hard to put the brakes on before he went completely into a skid as Peter pulled his head back and looked at her.

''Raven, maybe I should go—'' He was aware of his own blood pumping wildly through his veins, aware of desire chewing huge holes into him. But that was no excuse for what he was allowing to happen.

Disappointment drenched her. But she couldn't force him into this. It had to be something he wanted. In her heart, she knew what he was going through, knew that he had to be afraid. She certainly was because she was taking a huge risk. Reaching out to someone. Making herself vulnerable to someone. She was friendly, outgoing, but there was always a part of herself she kept locked away. Until now.

She could only step out so far on the tightrope on her own.

"The choice is yours," she whispered.

It was and, heaven help him, he was probably making the wrong one.

He found her mouth again, kissed her again. Kissed her so that all the logical thoughts that assaulted his brain didn't have a prayer of getting through.

Her heart raced so fast, she was afraid it would pop out of her chest. She put every bit of passion she felt into her kiss.

And then he was picking her up into his arms, sweeping her off her feet.

"Where?" The single word was husky, echoing into her very soul.

She pointed to her door. Everything within her was on heightened alert, a step away from being singed in the fire that had already begun to consume her.

Her heart had somehow gotten tangled up without her realizing it. In her effort to save the man, to make him feel again, she'd lost herself. More than anything, she was afraid she was allowing herself to make a mistake. But either way, there would be regrets. Regrets if she didn't allow this to happen.

Regrets if she did.

She knew she'd rather have a piece of something, than feel remorse over emptiness.

As they crossed the threshold to her room, she wound her arms around his neck and kissed him harder, praying that the night that shimmered in front of her would last forever.

Chapter Twelve

He'd always been a slow lover, a patient lover. But it had been so long since he had been, either. There was an urgency inside of him, drumming its fingers against his soul, that drove him on, made him want to run where he would have walked.

It took almost superhuman control to rein himself in even moderately. He couldn't allow the demands that battered against him to break free and take him over entirely.

Setting Raven down on the floor in front of her bed, he felt behind him for the door and closed it. He didn't want to spend a second not looking at her. She was beautiful and right now, everything he wanted.

That was why it almost killed him to say it, but he knew, in all good conscience, that he had to do it, that he had to force the words out of his mouth. "I can stop."

"But then I'd have to kill you," she whispered. Up against him, she twined her body around his. All their parts fit together so well, as if they were two halves of a whole. She looked up at him, her face less than an inch away from his. Her eyes were serious. "Do you want to stop?"

"Oh God, no." He had to be truthful. Stopping now was the last thing he wanted.

"Good, because I don't want you to, either." Her breath seductively caressed his skin.

It was all that was needed. Instincts took over, instincts that seemed to wiggle their way out of the crypt he'd placed them in. He hadn't been with a woman since Lisa. Hadn't wanted to be with a woman since Lisa. He'd never been a man who had been driven by sexual appetites. That had never been foremost in his life. Granted, before Lisa, he'd slept with a few women, but not nearly as many as a man his age might have.

To him sex was secondary. First there had to be some kind of feeling, some kind of a connection. Sex for sex's sake had always seemed so meaningless to him. A waste of time and energy that could have been better devoted to something else. Something fulfilling. Like saving lives, or at the very least, bettering them.

The very first time he had seen Raven, she had gotten to him. Gotten under his skin, into his brain. He'd spent more time denying that he wanted her than he had doing almost anything else since the day he met her.

The time for denial was past.

And maybe, after this was over, he could put it behind him and get back to life as he knew it. Life with some kind of purpose, some kind of direction and things like passions and desires would once again become just words in a dictionary. Words that had nothing to do with him.

But first, he needed to make love with her.

He took the edges of the short, light blue sweater that hardly brushed against the top of her belt and raised them up over her head. He discarded it without a glance, finding that what he'd suspected was true. She wasn't wearing a bra.

With hands that were already tingling, he gently cupped her breasts. The very act made something in his gut tighten so hard, taking in a deep breath was almost impossible. Seeing her like this didn't help steady his pulse, either.

Her skin felt like silk. He heard her raspy breath against his ear. It drove him on, stirring him more, making him wonder how he'd managed to hold himself in check for even this long.

Slipping his fingers in along the waistband of her jeans, Peter felt her stomach quiver beneath his touch. She was breathing harder now. And then he realized that the sound he heard was coming from him. His breathing mimicked hers. Raven stirred his blood, heating it, making it surge through his veins with a degree of energy he'd long since forgotten.

He realized that while he'd been undressing her, she'd been undoing his shirt. Pushing it off his shoulders, she turned her attention to the button on his pants. Within seconds, his own clothes had slipped off, joining hers on the floor.

Guiding her to him, he stepped aside, leaving the heap on the floor.

She had on thong underwear with a bevy of colorful, tiny butterflies fluttering strategically around the rim. He placed the heel of his hand there, feeling her warmth as it generated through. The warmth traveled up his arm, all but setting him on fire.

Peter caught her to him, kissing her over and over again. Each kiss brought them closer to the bed until they tumbled down onto it, their bodies a mass of tangled, questing limbs.

His hands slid over her tight body, glorying in the touch, the feel of it. He worked away her thong, drawing it down the length of her. Part of him didn't even believe this was real. She was like something out of a dream. He slid his hand along her torso, as if trying to commit every curve, every dip to memory.

When he touched her breast again, he felt the erratic rhythm beneath his fingers.

"I can feel your heart," he murmured. Rather than withdraw his hand, he spread his fingers, splaying them over her breast.

"Good, it's still there," she quipped between a shower of small kisses she rained down on him. "I was afraid it had exploded."

Her breath along his face was incredibly seductive. Each word tasted better than anything had a right to. The urgency to take her grew and his struggle for control increased in tandem. He fought for it every inch of the way.

His touch was making her crazy. She could almost feel all the thoughts go spinning out of her head. She'd never felt this out of control before, this disoriented and yet so focused. Every pinprick of attention was centered on the man whose body was making hers sing. She loved the feel of his hard muscles as he loomed over her, the touch of his hand as he caressed rather than claimed.

He was gentler than she'd thought he'd be. So gentle that he captured her completely, took away all her defenses and made her far more vulnerable than she would have willingly allowed herself to be.

There was no question in her mind. She was his.

Just like that.

It was incredible to her that she trusted him to this extent, this man she hadn't even known a month ago. She'd trusted him with what amounted to her brother's future and now, she was trusting him not to hurt her.

It was a huge burden to place upon a man.

She doubted that he knew.

Doubted that she could have even put it into words right now. All she really knew was that he had lit this fire inside her and the flames were licking up and down her very sides, consuming her.

Anticipation rose within her as Peter kissed every part of her, succeeding in raising her body temperature with each pass of his lips. It took everything she had not to cry out from the sensations that slammed around within her. Even though her bedroom was several doors away from Blue's, she didn't want to take a chance on her voice carrying, didn't want to take a chance of waking up the boy.

Her mouth sealed to his once again, Raven arched her body against him, silently asking for the final moment of fulfillment. Moist, throbbing and anxious, she didn't know just how much longer she was going to be able to hold out. She felt herself tottering on the brink for what seemed like eternity.

She twisted and turned, urging him to take her. To become one with her. Her fingernails dug into the muscles on his back as he kissed the hollow of her throat, raising a symphony of sensations all through her.

And then he pivoted on his elbows, his eyes holding hers for a moment. She wished she knew what he was thinking, but was afraid to ask, afraid to break apart the moment. She felt his knee between her thighs. Her pulse racing, she opened for him.

With one deep thrust, he was inside of her. When she looked, she saw that his eyes were closed. Was that because he was imagining his wife? She didn't know and the uncertainty hurt. But then she quickly set aside the question with its accompanying pain, not wanting to ruin the moment. She needed this. On whatever terms it was given, she needed this.

They moved together, the tempo growing more and more urgent as the race with only winners was run. And just when she thought that all air was depleted from her lungs, the final crescendo came, sweeping her away.

She felt his arms tighten around her. It was as if he were trying to absorb her into his very being. And then, ever so slowly, the intensity abated. His hold loosened. His body, taut like a bow only a heartbeat before, seemed to sink into hers. She gasped for breath as her heart hammered out the last strains of Tchaikovsky's "1812 Overture."

Somewhere in the back of her brain, the words "YES" echoed.

* * *

What the hell had he done?

The question pounded in his brain, creating no answers. He'd just breached every ethic, betrayed every oath he'd ever sworn, whether it was out loud or just to himself. What had possessed him to do it, to do this?

The answer was simple.

She had.

Even now, with senses returning, he couldn't deny that she felt wondrously good against him.

But remorse, laced with chains of guilt, bore down on him, growing heavier by the second. Moving off her, Peter looked down at her face, a myriad of recriminations crowding through his mind.

She could see it all—the doubt, the regret, the confusion—it was all there in his face as obvious as daylight. Desperately, Raven searched for the tiniest sign that somewhere within all that angst there existed just the smallest sliver of joy. Just a dot to match the joy that surged within her own breast.

She couldn't find it.

"Disappointed?" she finally asked him.

He stared at her for a second, the single word not computing. "Disappointed?" he echoed in disbelief. "Is that what you think?"

Given the look on his face, what other conclusion could she come to? Raven thought. "Well, you don't exactly look like a man who's just made love with someone. You look like a man who's just been sentenced to twenty years of hard labor beneath a merciless sun."

"I'm not disappointed," he told her firmly. "At least, not in you."

"I don't understand."

He tried to explain, but he didn't know where to start. "I've broken more rules than I can count."

"Maybe you should stop counting, then." She cupped his cheek with her hand, forcing him to look at her. Very lightly, she brushed her lips against his. "This isn't about rules, Peter. It's about kindred souls."

The simple kiss created a sweetness within him. He could feel it pouring through his veins. "Kindred souls? You and me?"

Her eyes smiled up into his before she even answered. "Yes."

His soul was black, hers was white. Where did she possibly find any similarities? Unable to resist, he ran the back of his hand along her skin. And felt himself growing excited again.

"And how do you see that?"

She hit only the highlights. What she felt went deeper than that. "We've both been hurt, both lost people we loved in traumatic accidents."

That didn't begin to make them kindred spirits. "The doctor who assisted at your brother's surgery lost his wife in a car accident five years ago. I've never made love with him. Never even been tempted to."

There was a whole host of things that made them kindred spirits, but she didn't want to belabor the fact. Right now, she just wanted them to enjoy one another. She nodded her approval of his comment.

"Humor, good. There's still a chance your soul hasn't completely dried up. As a matter of fact—" she smiled at him, drawing a tiny circle along his chest with her fingertip "—I think I can pretty much guarantee it."

He was being sarcastic. This wasn't a time for humor, it was a time for introspection. More than that, it was a time to get hold of himself.

Easing his body away from hers, Peter sat up, the sheet pooling around his lap. "I think maybe I should go."

Raven sighed. She couldn't very well tie him to the bed. "Only if you promise to stop feeling guilty."

"I'm not guilty." Peter pressed his lips together. He'd bitten off the words as he spoke. They both knew he was lying.

Raven sat up beside him, unmindful of the sheet that fell to her waist. He couldn't help thinking that she was magnificent in her lack of self-consciousness. His body tightened just looking at her.

"Then what's this?" she asked, sliding her finger

along the furrow between his brow. ''People who aren't guilty don't look as if they're about to shoot thunder from their brow.''

He caught her hand in his. ''Got an answer for everything, don't you?''

The smile was slow, almost feline as it curved her mouth. ''I try.''

He was feeling it again. Feeling that almost insurmountable urge to kiss her again, to hold her and to make love with her as if he hadn't already done so.

What had come over him? He didn't understand this change, this need that had taken him prisoner. It was as if he was afraid that the first time had been nothing more than a mere hallucination on his part and he needed to be convinced that it had been real.

He needed to make love with her again to assure himself that it hadn't been just a dream.

He confused the hell out of himself. More than that, this feeling scared him, as well. When he'd been with Lisa, he hadn't known the kind of risk he was taking, didn't know that losing someone you cared about could rip the very heart out of your chest. But he knew now. So what was he still doing here, sitting beside Raven? Wanting her?

So many emotions ran riot through him that he couldn't begin to sort them out. And each and every one of them began and ended with her.

He knew he should leave. Instead he found himself tugging Raven onto his lap, kissing the hollow of her neck, feasting on the smooth, creamy skin along her shoulder. He just couldn't get enough of her. Every kiss gave birth to another until his inclination to resist her vanished.

As he kissed her mouth, he could feel her smile against his lips. A smile grew within him. He knew there would be no peace for him until he made love with Raven again.

Peter opened his eyes.

At first, he thought it was the middle of the night. The bedroom was still cloaked in darkness. There was still time for him to make good his escape. But as he turned, about to get up, he found that the place beside him was empty. The next moment he realized that Raven was standing by the foot of the bed.

Her smile was bright and warming, instantly reminding him of the night they had just spent. "Hi, I didn't mean to wake you."

Peter blinked, trying to rouse his mind and get it started. Raven was fully dressed. How much time had passed? How long had he been sleeping?

Adrenaline filled his body as the fight-or-flight syndrome took hold. The cobwebs disappeared from his brain. "What time is it?"

"Six-thirty." In response, Peter instantly bolted upright like a jack-in-the-box that had been over-wound. She dropped down by his feet on the bed, concerned. ''What's the matter?''

His escape route temporarily blocked, he considered sliding out on the other side. ''I should have left hours ago.''

She cocked her head, studying him. Thinking how cute he looked with a stubble on his face. ''Why, what happened hours ago?''

About to get up, Peter realized that he was still naked beneath the sheet that was draped haphazardly over him. Holding it to him, he leaned over the side of the bed and picked up the pants that he'd kicked aside last night. Heaven only knew where his underwear was.

In answer to her question, he told her the first thing that popped into his agitated head. ''I've got an early surgery scheduled.''

He was avoiding her eyes. ''Not before six-thirty,'' she was willing to bet. *If then,* she added silently. ''Want breakfast?'' She rose to her feet, giving him clear access to the floor. ''I'm a terrific short-order cook.''

Working beneath the sheet, he slid the pants on, then worked on getting the zipper up. ''No, I'll get something at the hospital.''

She placed her hand on his shoulder, momentarily holding him in place. ''This isn't the scene of a crime, Peter. You don't have to escape before someone sees you.''

But it was. It *was* the scene of a crime. A crime against her, against the memory of his wife, and the sooner he left, the better it would be all around.

''I didn't mean for—''

Peter stopped abruptly. How the hell was he going to phrase this?

He didn't have to finish. Raven could read between the lines. ''That's too bad,'' she told him quietly, ''because I did. I meant for it all to happen. I never thought I could, but I did.''

On his feet beside the bed, Peter looked at her. For the first time, he examined the situation from her perspective instead of his own.

''Why wouldn't you be able to…?'' What words did he use? *Make love with someone? Sleep with someone?* Stumped, he just let the sentence die ignobly between them, hoping she would silently fill in the blanks.

''The words you might not know you're looking for are 'care about someone else.' Why would I think I wasn't able to care about someone else? The answer's simple. Because I didn't want to get hurt again, didn't want to risk losing again.'' And then she paused, once again reading his expression. ''Don't look so frightened, Peter, there's no responsibility attached to what happened between you and me last night.''

But he had seized upon what she'd said first. That she hadn't thought she could care about anyone again. If that was true, then there was only one conclusion to be drawn. "You mean, there's no one in your life?"

She had a feeling he didn't realize he was insulting her. "I wouldn't have slept with you if there was."

This didn't make any sense to him. She was young, beautiful and, if the magazines were to be believed, one of the richest women in the country. A perfect trifecta from most men's standpoint. "And why isn't there anyone in your life?"

She was surprised that he, of all people, had to ask something like that. "Because, like you, I've been afraid to let myself open up."

Yes, he knew what she'd said about their being kindred souls, but he hadn't thought she really believed it. "You?" he echoed incredulously.

"Me," she confirmed. And then she smiled a little wistfully. "We're not that different, you and I. The heart gets hurt, the heart backs off, it's as simple as that."

Going to the door, she stopped to look at him over her shoulder. "Get dressed. Breakfast will be waiting for you downstairs."

"Don't bother," he called after her. He just wanted to leave the premises as soon as possible.

"No bother," she quipped, closing the door behind her.

* * *

Despite their last exchange, Peter still tried to make good his getaway. It took him exactly ten minutes to find his underwear—it was under the bed where it had somehow gotten kicked last night—and get properly dressed. The hallway, when he entered it, was empty. He figured he was home free.

But he hadn't counted on the boy.

Blue was waiting for him at the bottom of the stairs when he came down. Sitting on the last step, Blue rose to his feet before he could reach him.

Peter stifled an exasperated sigh. Was he going to be the target of questions? After all, he was wearing the suit he'd had on last night. "Why aren't you asleep?"

Small shoulders rose and fell carelessly in response. "Raven and I always get up early. She told me to bring you to the kitchen when you were dressed."

The front door was a simple sprint away. He eyed it. "I have to get going."

"She said you'd say that. She told me not to pay attention." Blue wrapped his fingers around his hand and tugged. "C'mon, she's made French toast and it's really good."

Unable to do anything else without causing at least a minor scene, Peter allowed himself to be dragged into the kitchen.

Chapter Thirteen

Blue brought him into the kitchen. ‘‘Here he is, Raven.’’

Raven looked at both of them over her shoulder. She wore a blue apron over her clothes and was probably the sexiest chef Peter had ever seen.

‘‘Make yourself comfortable,’’ she told him, then added with a smile as she went back to cooking, ‘‘Or, barring that, sit down.’’

‘‘I can’t,’’ he protested, although not nearly as adamantly or firmly as he wanted.

‘‘Sure you can.’’ She reached for the powdered sugar and drizzled it all over her creation. Turning with plate in hand, she walked over to the table.

"Just bend your knees and let yourself collapse into the chair."

Muttering something under his breath, he did as she instructed.

"See how easy that was?" Her grin went straight into his gut, piercing it. Piercing another organ vital to his survival, as well.

Without meaning to, he absorbed the sounds and smells within the kitchen. And the life that it represented. He could see himself getting too used to this, too comfortable with it. The last hurdle had been cleared last night when they'd made love.

Raven made it much too easy for him to slip into this life that beckoned irresistibly to him. A life that had such strong echoes of the past. This world reminded him of the happiest days of his life. More than being a surgeon, Peter knew in his secret heart of hearts that he was meant to be a husband, a father. Both roles had been cruelly wrenched from him with a finality that had all but shattered him and now, here he was, glimpsing the past, stupidly thinking that maybe, just maybe, it could be his future, too.

He couldn't go that way, he thought fiercely. Couldn't allow himself to think like that. Even if everything went well, taking this path that loomed so temptingly in front of him would leave him open to a world of pain. He just couldn't subject himself to that again. This time, he wouldn't come out whole.

He knew it as surely as he knew his name. And yet, she was making it so hard to walk away, to even now, reclaim his life. He had to be firm, had to move back from the step he'd taken by coming here last night. Peter looked at the boy on his left.

"How do you like Dr. Rhys?" He meant the question to segue into the topic of Rhys as his doctor and not him. Somehow he wanted to make it clear that this bogus visit was the only one of its kind. He'd been weak, allowed himself to stray from the path he'd prescribed for himself.

Not the man of iron that he saw himself to be, Peter thought.

Blue shifted on his chair, as if uncomfortable. He had been raised to be polite, but he'd also been raised not to lie. "He's not you."

Peter wasn't comfortable with compliments, even genuine ones coming from a pint-size patient. He approached the comment as if it was intended literally. "No, of course not, but—"

"I think he's trying to tell you that he'd rather be seeing you," Raven said as she placed a heaping plate of French toast in front of him. She then sat herself and looked directly at Peter. "And so would I."

The sentence was open-ended, just vague enough for him to wonder if she meant that strictly professionally, or if she was telling him that she wanted to see him again socially.

That was just wishful thinking on his part, Peter upbraided himself. A woman like Raven Songbird didn't need to seek out companionship. It sought her out. She had the world at her feet.

To convince himself that she and he were worlds apart, he'd done a little reading up on her. She wasn't just a beautiful figurehead at her parents' company, she'd become very hands-on within its operation in the last five years. He'd learned that her degree had been in business and she had obviously been a good student. Under her tutelage, the company's profits had more than tripled in the past five years and she had taken them into new markets. Songbird clothes were not only sold in certain department stores, but through its own retail outlets and were also sold on the Internet.

A woman who was savvy, beautiful and rich could have any man she chose. There was no reason for him to believe that she would choose him. Which made leaving easier.

Or should have.

Stalling just a little, he took a bite of the French toast and discovered that she continued to amaze him. Raven was a woman of many talents. His taste buds were smiling even if he wasn't. "I've already told you that—"

Raven sat, her hands wrapped around her oversize coffee cup, watching her brother and her lover eat. Blue did so with unabashed relish. Peter was far more inhibited. She was going to have to work on that.

"Yes, I know," she said patiently. "You operate, Dr. Rhys holds hands." Leaning over the blue-pearl granite tabletop, she played her trump card. "I'll build another wing on to the hospital."

It was one hell of a bribe, he thought, and she made it without blinking an eye. "You really do like to get what you want, don't you?"

Her mouth curved. There was no denying she liked getting her way. But she always made sure no one was hurt in the process. It had been her edict ever since she could remember. "As long as I can do it nicely."

He knew he should be annoyed about this, that he should rebel against having his arm twisted. But he couldn't seem to work up the energy. "You've probably already called George."

She had and this was independent of anything he might ultimately say. But it suited her purpose to make him think that this wasn't a done deal yet. "It's on my schedule for things to do today."

Peter had some more of the French toast, fortifying himself. He looked at Blue, who appeared to be waiting for a decision. "I suppose, seeing as how this is actually for the greater good, I could see you in my office in about two weeks."

Blue beamed at him. "You could see me sooner than that."

He *wasn't* going to be told how to practice medicine, even by an overly intelligent child. "I don't really need to."

The moment he'd said it, he knew it was a lie. At least emotionally. Because he *did* need to see Blue. Needed to see them both, especially her. Which was why he couldn't.

Damn it, why couldn't he stick to his plan?

Blue shook his head, his straight black hair flying back and forth around his face. "No, I mean here." He met Peter's quizzical look. "I've got a birthday coming up on Saturday. Raven is throwing a big party for me. I'd like you to come."

The boy extended the invitation as cordially as if he was thirty-five and sitting in some exclusive men's club, talking over brandy. The only thing that gave away his age, other than his size, was the glint in the boy's bright blue eyes.

Looking on silently for once, Raven saw Peter hesitate. Saw an excuse coming. Leaning to the side, she took her brother's face in one hand and turned it so that Peter could get the full benefit of the view.

"How can you possibly say no to this face?" she asked.

She was right. He couldn't. Not to Blue's face and not to hers.

But saying yes didn't mean he had to actually show up, he thought. He needed a safety net to save him from the huge fall he knew was coming. He was a doctor, emergencies were part of the general scenario. There was a last minute way out.

"All right," he conceded, "what time is it?"

"Saturday," she repeated in case he forgot. "It starts at four."

Peter nodded, mentally making plans accordingly.

He arrived at five.

He very nearly hadn't come at all. He'd been resisting the idea of showing up for the past three days, resisting it right up until the time that he'd pulled up into her driveway and found himself surrendering his vehicle to a valet who had apparently been on the look-out for him. The moment he had approached the winding driveway, a young man in a navy-blue jacket and black slacks came hurrying over to him.

Leaning into the driver's side, the valet placed his hands on the door. "Ms. Songbird's been expecting you, Doctor."

The woman was thorough, he'd give her that. If he pulled out of the driveway now, it would be nothing short of a cowardly act. He hated looking like a coward. Whether he was or not didn't matter, it was the appearance that counted. Besides, Raven had made good on her promise and called George. The upshot was that Songbird, Inc. would be footing the bill for the addition of another wing to the hospital. It was a good thing, seeing as how the children's ward was already vastly overcrowded.

All things considered, Peter knew he was required to make at least a cursory appearance at this party.

Ten minutes, he promised himself as he got out.

Before he could say anything about keeping the vehicle near the front, the valet had taken the keys from him, hopped into his car and driven it out of sight. So much for an easy, unnoticed escape.

Tucking the boy's gift under his arm, Peter braced himself and walked up to the front door.

There was no need to ring the bell.

It seemed as if there was some kind of a relay system that existed between the valet and the maid in charge of admitting guests. The front door swung open the moment he stepped in front of it.

A petite dark-haired woman in an old-fashioned maid's uniform smiled a greeting at him. But Peter wasn't really looking at her. He was looking at everyone else within view. Directly behind the maid was a crowd scene that had been lifted straight out of what appeared to be a rendition of *Saturday Night Fever.*

Everyone wore costumes straight out of that era.

Now that he thought of it, the maid's uniform looked as if it could have come from that time, too.

He didn't belong here.

Making a decision, he thrust the gift he was carrying at the woman. "Would you give this to Blue Songbird for me?"

Forced to take the box, the woman stared at it. "But don't you want to—"

He wasn't even going to allow her to finish. He already knew what she was going to ask. "No."

He didn't want to. Didn't want to be here, didn't want to make a fool of himself because of this woman.

This was a mistake.

God, he wished he had never come here tonight. He knew that Raven was far too decent a person to cancel her pledge just because he hadn't shown up.

Without another word to the maid, Peter turned on his heel, striding away from the house.

His getaway was quite possibly the shortest lived on record.

"Peter, wait!"

He stiffened.

Raven.

He would have recognized her voice anywhere. The house appeared to have more people crammed into it than had been on the set of the movie *The Ten Commandments.* How had she seen him?

Reluctantly he turned around again and saw her

hurrying toward him. It was a crisp November afternoon. The wind fanned her hair out around her and whipped through her wide skirt, making the fabric cling against her body.

Making him remember the other night.

His mouth grew dry.

He nodded toward the house. She hadn't bothered to close the door. ''You didn't tell me it was a costume party.''

''I didn't think you'd come if I did.''

His eyes narrowed. ''I don't like standing out.''

Wearing a peasant blouse with billowing sleeves, she hooked her arm through his. He didn't know which was more seductive to him, her Navajo side or her Gypsy side. ''You'd stand out if they used you for the bed where the guests are tossing their coats,'' she informed him.

''I'm supposed to be saying things like that to you,'' he pointed out.

She stopped at the front door, turning toward him. Her breast brushed against his arm and desire stirred within him. ''No one's stopping you.''

He tried to keep his mind focused. The noise from inside the mansion wafted toward him. ''Raven, I can't go in there like this.''

''No problem, I have a costume set aside for you.'' As gently as her brother had the other day, she tugged him into the house.

He should have known. Still, he tried to make

her see things his way one last time. "I don't like dressing up."

She made no effort to hide her grin. It slyly spread across the corners of her mouth. "If you come naked, there might be a problem."

"Raven—"

Releasing his arm, she threaded her fingers through his. She began to lead him up the stairs. "It'll be fun," she promised.

He had no choice but to follow in her wake. "Not for me."

On the stairs, she stopped for a second to look at him over her shoulder. "Then for me."

"It's you," she declared less than fifteen minutes later when he emerged out of the sumptuous black marble bathroom and into one of the umpteen guest bedrooms wearing the outfit she'd presented to him.

How she'd known his size was beyond him. If it had been too tight or too large, he would have had a way out. But it fit perfectly. All three pieces. He had on bell bottom jeans, a flowered shirt that seemed to be made of the same fabric as her skirt, topped off by a vest with fringes that went from the middle of his rib cage down well past his hips.

"Only if I've become seriously schizophrenic," he told her grudgingly. The wardrobe doors were mirrored. He glanced at his reflection and was surprised at what he saw. He'd lived in three-piece suits and surgical scrubs for so long, he'd forgotten that there *was* any other clothing available. "I suppose I should count myself lucky that you didn't make me wear a long-haired wig."

She grinned, moving next to him. The thought had crossed her mind, but she really did like the look of his own hair. Thick and black. She ran her fingers through it to tease him.

"I pick my battles."

He looked at the two of them standing together. It was oddly reminiscent of one of the photographs he'd seen of her parents in a magazine article he'd found on the Internet. Raven looked a great deal like her mother, Rowena, he realized.

The next moment, Raven leaned into him. Taking hold of his shirt, she pulled his head down to her level and brushed her lips against his. "Thanks for being such a good sport."

He laughed shortly as she released her hold on his shirt. "Did I have a choice?"

She looked at him for a long moment. "You always had a choice." And then she smiled again. "This means a lot to Blue."

He had yet to even see the boy. "There must be a hundred people out there—"

"A hundred and twenty," she corrected.

"I don't think he'd even miss me."

"Trust me," she told him, carefully hanging up the clothes he had arrived in, "he'd miss you." She placed his suit and shirt into the closet for the time being. Even as she did so, she couldn't help wondering if he was going to spend the night. ''Blue's got radar when it comes to things like that.''

Her blouse slid seductively from her shoulder. He blocked a very real desire to press a kiss to the skin he saw exposed. ''Takes after his sister, I guess.''

Turning toward him again, she grinned as she tugged her blouse back into place.

Maybe it was the costume, or maybe he had just taken leave of his senses. It wasn't clear to him, but whatever the reason, he gave in to his impulse and pulled Raven to him. The surprised then pleased expression on her face only served to fuel the desire that grew in his veins. He brought his mouth to hers.

Though he would have wanted it to continue forever, he allowed the kiss to go on only a moment, afraid that what was happening inside of him would get the best of him, pushing him in directions he told himself he had no intentions of going again.

He knew he was lying about the last part.

The look in her eyes was nothing short of abject delight as she looked at him. ''You're loosening up already.''

He shrugged, avoiding her eyes. ''Must be the costume,'' he muttered.

He didn't have to look at her to know she was grinning. ''Must be.''

* * *

He really hadn't planned on having fun. Never much of a joiner, Peter had been the man who perpetually lived on the outside. It didn't bother him. Being on the outside had become familiar to him. Safe. If you weren't close to anything, you didn't risk anything. Eventually, he felt awkward in any other position.

But being on the outside was not an option tonight. Raven seemed bent on infusing him into this party she'd thrown for her brother. She never left his side and made it a point to introduce him to everyone who crossed their path. She introduced him as the neurosurgeon who had saved Blue from living a life confined to a wheelchair and allowed, after linking her hand with his, everyone else to make their own conclusions after that.

Peter watched their responses with growing amusement as interest entered and flared within people's eyes when they covertly looked from her to him.

It wasn't lost on Raven, either. At one point she raised herself up on her toes and whispered against his ear, "I think they think we're an item."

Because he wanted to have her elaborate, he played dumb. "An item?"

She nodded. "You know, together." Her eyes smiled into his. "A couple."

A couple. How long had it been since the word had had anything to do with him? It sounded almost seductive now. Maybe he shouldn't have that last glass of wine. But wine wasn't going to his head, he thought. She was. Everything about her was. "Maybe you should set them straight."

Her face was a study in pure innocence as she looked at him. "What should I tell them?"

"That I'm Blue's doctor." But then, he reminded himself, she'd already told everyone that.

Raven cocked her head. Her blouse had slipped from her shoulder again and it was bare as her hair brushed along it. Peter felt his stomach tightening. "Is that all?"

He pretended to think it over. "I'm trapped in a time warp from the seventies?" he guessed.

He could feel her smile inside his chest. Feel her warmth as it touched him. "Anything else?"

Suddenly he wanted to get out of here. To take her with him and spend the remainder of the night making love with her. To savor for all time. But he couldn't say that to her. He could hardly say that to himself.

"I don't know," he finally admitted.

It felt as if she'd taken another step closer to him, even though she hadn't moved a muscle. "Should I get back to you on that?"

He needed to warn her away, before it was too late for both of them. He didn't want her thinking he could give her something he couldn't. "Raven, I'm hollow inside."

"Hollow things are just begging for something to fill them," she told him softly.

He shook his head. This just wasn't going to work. "Look—"

But just then the band that she had hired began to play a slow song. Her eyes lit up as the first strains drifted through the air. "Always and Forever."

"Listen. That was my parents' favorite song. My dad asked my mom to marry him while they were dancing to this." Taking him by the hand, she started leading him to the area that had been cleared as a dance floor. "Dance with me, Peter?" she asked suddenly. "You don't have to ask me to marry you, but I really would love to dance."

"I don't dance." The words were uttered to the back of her head.

As usual, she didn't accept his protest. "You can shift from foot to foot, can't you?"

"Yes, but—"

She turned around to face him, her hands out, waiting for his to take them. "Good, then you can dance. Trust me. Slow dances are just moving your feet from side to side. They're really just about holding someone to you. Unless you don't want to do that."

He didn't answer her. Instead he took her into his arms and began to sway. If she wanted to call it dancing, fine. He called it heaven.

Chapter Fourteen

Peter didn't leave.

It was well into the evening before the last stragglers finally left the party. The birthday boy had been going strong throughout it all, displaying more energy than any three boys his age combined. Blue said it was because he'd turned eight.

But the minute the last guest was out the door, he seemed to collapse. Anyone looking at him would have seen one very tired kid.

Raven turned away from the door and looked at him, her heart melting. He was trying so hard to be all grown up. *Don't hurry the process too much, Blue. Be little for as long as you can.*

''Want me to carry some of your loot upstairs, Tiger?'' she asked, ruffling Blue's hair.

He picked up three action figures that had caught his fancy the moment he'd unwrapped them. They'd come from his best friend, Chuck.

''No, that's okay.'' He looked at the collection of toys and games he'd amassed. They were all spread out in the family room, where the kids had gone to play while the adults had danced and pretended they were kids. ''Can I put them away in the morning?''

Trying to keep a serious face, Raven looked at her watch. ''Well, you still have two hours left to be king.'' She executed a deep curtsy. ''Whatever you wish, Blue.'' She saw Peter look at her quizzically. ''It's his birthday, he gets to makes the rules—within reason,'' she added with a wink sent her brother's way.

Blue seemed too tired to notice. He was already heading toward the stairs and his bedroom, an action figure in each hand, and one tucked under his arm.

''I'll be up in a minute to tuck you in,'' Raven told him.

Blue spared her a single look. ''I'm eight.'' If he meant the statement as a protest, he wasn't altogether convincing.

''And still tuckable,'' she called after him before turning toward Peter. She couldn't get over how good he looked. But she knew he was probably miserable. That he'd endured this for her—and Blue—meant a great deal. "I imagine you can't wait to get out of those clothes."

Peter stared at her. "What?" His eyes immediately glanced toward the stairs to see if Blue had overheard her comment. But if the boy had, it hadn't registered. He was still trudging up the spiral staircase.

Raven pressed her lips together in order not to laugh. "And into your own," she clarified. Although peeling him out of his clothes was definitely not a bad idea, she thought.

"Yeah, right," he muttered, slightly embarrassed.

He figured that it was rather obvious what he was thinking. What he had been thinking all evening long. That he wanted her, wanted to be with her away from this crowd. How could he *not* feel that way, seeing as how she was at his side all evening, her body brushing against his, the fragrance in her hair all but seducing him. When they had danced together, it had been all he could do not to kiss her.

But he was a private person. And what he was feeling right now was very, very private.

"The bedroom where you left your clothes is over here." She began to lead the way.

It was a big house, but he wasn't completely without a sense of direction. "I remember."

Ah, she was obviously treading on his manly art of pathfinding, she thought, backing away.

"Okay." She changed direction. "Then I'll go see to Blue."

As he passed the unwrapped gifts, he had to ask her. "The presents Blue got…"

She stopped, looking at him. "Yes?"

He would have expected outlandishly expensive gifts being bestowed on the boy. Instead, Blue seemed rather happy to have toys that could have easily been found in any toy store.

"I'm surprised that he just got…" His voice trailed off.

"Normal gifts?" she supplied. "Because, despite the fact that my little brother's super-intelligent, he's mercifully just a normal little boy under all that. I asked anyone who wanted to spend a lot of money to donate it to a charity in his name. The last thing I want is for Blue to get spoiled. Living in this house, knowing there's half an empire waiting for him when he comes of age, is hard enough to deal with. For as long as possible, I want him remaining sweet and innocent."

She looked so serious, like a crusader espousing a cause near and dear to her heart. He fought the urge to take her into his arms. "Like you."

The serious expression melted as Raven smiled at him. Her eyes danced. "We both know I'm not all *that* innocent."

Unable to refrain, Peter cupped her cheek. ''I'm looking forward to that part.''

She pulled back, even though she didn't want to. ''I've got a little brother to tuck in. Wait for me.''

As if he could do anything else, he thought, watching her hurry away.

Despite the profusion of costumes dating back to another decade, the evening was not about pretenses. They both knew he was staying. He didn't even bother trying to lie to himself by pretending that he was leaving once he had changed his clothes.

Nothing but a full-fledged emergency at the hospital could make him walk away from her tonight.

She was back just as he'd finished changing out of the costume and into his own clothes. She knocked on the door so softly, he almost thought it was his imagination.

''Come in.''

Raven peeked in before entering. She saw the bell bottoms, shirt and vest carefully folded over the back of one of the chairs. He was back in uniform, she thought. ''Feel better?''

Tie in hand, he turned to look at her. She was still wearing the same outfit she'd had on during the party. Rather than date her, it made her look appealingly timeless.

''More like me,'' he confessed.

Crossing to him, Raven framed his face between her hands. Very lightly, she moved them along his cheeks. "Yes, it definitely feels like you," she murmured. Rising on her toes, she lightly pressed her lips against his, then pulled away again, as if weighing something in her mind. "Tastes like you, too."

"Are you sure?" He fit his hands on the swell of her hips. "Maybe you need another sample."

Taking hold of his tie, she slid it from his hand and tossed it aside. "I don't want a sample," she told him, her eyes never leaving his. "I want the main course."

"It's heating up even as we speak." Raven laughed then, softly, lightly, tantalizing him with the sound. He tugged her closer. Pulling the peasant blouse off her shoulder, he kissed it. "I've been wanting to do that all evening."

She could feel desire taking hold of her, its warm, probing fingers inserting themselves everywhere. Raven pressed against him. She could feel his body heat, feel it mingling with hers.

"What else have you been wanting to do?"

"This." As gently as he could, he pulled her blouse up over her head, then let it fall to the rug. This time, she was wearing a small, white lace bra.

But only for a moment.

It went the way of the blouse. In a heartbeat, he was covering the area with his hands instead of any fabric. Adrenaline began to surge through him, going in all directions at once. Pounding, demanding. Remembering.

"You shouldn't have gotten dressed," she murmured against his neck as she brushed her lips along his skin and made him crazy. "I'm only going to have to undress you."

Peter had no idea why hearing that suddenly made him feel weak in his knees, but it did. Something stirred within him, stirred hard. He found himself wanting her with a passion that was almost impossible to contain.

It took extreme control not to tear the clothes off his own body but to stand there instead as her long, cool fingers moved the jacket down along his arms, undid the buttons on first his vest, then his shirt, and slowly peeled them away from his body. By the time she got to his slacks, he felt as if he was going to burst.

He molded his hands over hers, hurrying her along. "You always this slow?"

Amusement lifted the corners of her mouth. She was loving this, loving his response, loving her own response to him.

Her arms around his neck, she cleaved to him. "No, just always this thorough."

He could almost feel her smile along his lips, even though there was a little bit of distance between them. When her hands rested on his hips, pushing away the finely tailored slacks, he pulled down her skirt and, with it, the small, inviting scrap that was her underwear.

Their nude bodies already slick with desire and anticipation, they returned to the playing field where all things were equal. Where the outside world did not intrude. He wanted nothing more than to touch her again, to explore her again, and silently, oh so silently, to commit again.

He made love to her with all the feeling that had burst free of its bounds, made love to her as if his very soul depended on it.

Because it did.

He hadn't had a soul in two years, he'd lost it the day he'd lost his family. And Raven had brought it back to him. Made him feel, made him afraid.

Made him alive.

Each time it was better than the last. Each time he took her, she was that much more convinced that this was as perfect as it could be.

And then it got better.

And somewhere along the line, amid the touches and the kisses, the fire and the passion, she knew. Knew that Peter Sullivan was the one. The one she wanted to spend the rest of her life with.

But that was something she was going to keep to herself.

* * *

Unlike the first time, he didn't stay the night. Because he wanted nothing more than to lie next to her.

He tried to tell himself that what he was experiencing was purely physical, that he'd passed some kind of rite of passage and had become like so many other men, just in need of a sexual release and nothing more.

The thought hung in front of him like the black lie it was even as he tried to convince himself of it.

Peter clung to the lie as he left her bed in the middle of the night, careful not to wake her. Because if he woke her, she would look at him with those eyes he adored and bring him back to her side without a word.

He was in jeopardy of going down for the third time and he had to do something to save himself. He was deathly afraid of the pain that was to be found at the end of the road.

Better not to feel anything than to feel that.

He almost had himself believing it as he slipped out the door.

Through hooded eyes, Raven had watched him get dressed, had watched him leave. Watched him as her heart grew heavier and heavier. She'd been hoping that, like her, he had emerged out the dark cave where he'd been hiding himself. Hiding his heart.

But they were two different people and while loving gave her hope, it obviously gave him despair.

Raven sighed, turning so that she stared up at the ceiling. Pulling the covers up around herself didn't take away the chill she felt. She knew Peter cared about her. In the ways of her mother's ancestors, she could sense it down to her very bones. She was never wrong when it came to things like this.

However, not being wrong didn't help make things turn out right. Didn't help convince him to remain with her. This was something that, ultimately, Peter was going to have to sort out for himself. She could only be there when he did.

Because her heart was not about to go anywhere.

''You look preoccupied.'' Dr. Harry Welles shifted, adjusting his hospital gown. He watched his star pupil step back from the bed. Peter had just come in to give him one last exam before the two of them were to meet again in the operating salon this morning. But rather than assist or supervise, Harry would spend the entirety of the operation anesthetized. It was an odd feeling.

Harry felt tired these days, the kind of tired that encompassed a lifetime. He promised himself a vacation once this was behind him.

He watched the strange, distant expression on Peter's face. ''Should I be worried?'' he finally prompted when there was no response.

Realizing that he'd let his thoughts drift off again, Peter frowned, annoyed at his lack of concentration. "No, this isn't about you." Because Harry deserved better, he added, "I'm sorry."

The expression on the other man's face told him that there was no need to be sorry. He'd never noticed before that Harry had patient eyes.

"Want to talk about it?" Harry offered.

What was there to say? Peter thought. He'd been trying to wean himself off Raven, to wean himself of his need for her and what she represented. "Not really."

Harry shook his head. "Bad sign, Peter. You should always find a way to talk."

Peter looked at him sharply. This didn't sound at all like the man he'd all but worshiped through his internship and residency. "You didn't."

"Exactly," Harry drove the point home. "That's why I know it's a bad sign."

He picked at the bedclothes, shaking his head again, this time at the irony that had brought him to this place. How many times had he been on the other side of the railing, assuring patients that everything was going to be fine and that they shouldn't worry? In this position, it was impossible *not* to worry.

Harry grasped the metal bar, looking down at the medical tag that encircled his wide wrist. It proclaimed to the entire world that he was not a doctor but a patient. "Funny thing about finding yourself on this side of the bed railings, you start to see things a lot differently. Start asking questions."

Peter thought he had a pretty good handle on what the man was probably going through. What he might be going through in his place. He'd already silently asked the question for Harry when faced with the man's diagnosis. "Like, why me?"

The question seemed to take Harry by surprise. "No, more like 'what the hell was I thinking?'"

Peter stared at the older man, confused. "Excuse me?"

"What was I thinking," Harry repeated, then added, "not having a life."

It still made no sense to Peter. Dr. Harry Welles was one of the most respected physicians in the country, not just by organizations but by his peers. He had an office full of awards to testify to that fact. "You have a life, Harry. A rich, full life." Harry's expression didn't change. Peter tried again. "You've helped so many people."

That was just the point and Harry seized it. "Yes, I have. I helped put them back together again so that they could enjoy life to the fullest." He sighed, looking suddenly older than his years. "But I never had the guts to do that myself." He looked at Peter, his eyes searching to see if he was getting through to him. "I fooled myself into thinking that my work was far too important to trivialize with the acquisition of a wife and family when the truth of it was, I was too much of a coward to put myself out there like that, to risk having the greatest experience of my life."

Peter had had no idea that his mentor felt this way. It was like finally unearthing the buried treasure after years of searching, only to find the chest filled not with gold but with air.

"And that is?"

"Falling in love. *Being* in love," Harry added fiercely. A fond look came into his eyes. "I was very envious of you for what you had."

He was talking about Lisa and Becky. Welles had been best man at his wedding. And Becky's godfather. Peter set his mouth grimly.

"I don't have it anymore."

"But you could." He made it a point to know things and he'd discovered that there was a spark between his protégé and the Songbird heiress. He'd heard nothing but good things about the woman. It gave him hope that Peter wouldn't make his mistakes. "I know that once this operation is behind me, I intend to try to make amends for being such a coward when it comes to life."

An almost boyish smile curved the older surgeon's lips. "There's this anesthesiologist I've been meaning to ask out. I think I will once you put me back together." It was a promise he was making to both himself and to Peter. Welles looked at him for a long moment. ''Don't wait until you're staring at your own mortality to do the right thing, Peter. ''Life deserves to be held on to with two hands, not observed meekly on the sidelines. Don't be like me,'' he insisted. ''Don't someday find yourself looking back over a forty-year career with nothing to show for it but awards and no one to share them with. No one to share your life with.''

Peter refused to believe that the man saw his entire life in terms of failure. ''That's just preoperative jitters talking.'' They'd both heard it before. It was the flip side of making promises to God in return for a safe outcome to the operation.

Harry put his hand over the man's he'd chosen to be his doctor. ''Doesn't make it any the less true. Think about what I said.''

Any further discussion was curtailed as a tall, pretty-looking nurse walked in, followed by a gregarious-looking male nurse.

Harry nodded at the pair. He knew them both. He made it a point to know everyone on the floor. It was one of the reasons everyone liked working with him.

''Well, I guess my ride's here.'' He took Peter's hand in his one last time. ''Think about what I said—'' Then he added with a smile, ''Just not during the operation. In there I want you thinking about nothing else but me.''

Peter laughed, trying to dispel the tension for

both of them. It was a serious operation with serious consequences. While he was flattered that the man had come to him to perform the surgery, he was still worried about the outcome.

"You've got it," he promised.

"As long as *you've* got it," Harry emphasized, then looked to the two other people in the private room. The space was the one concession he had requested because of his status in the hospital. He didn't feel up to sharing his condition and his uneasiness with any strangers. "Okay, boys and girls, time to show the old man what you're all made of." The nurses flanked him on either side of the bed, mobilizing it by taking the brakes off all four wheels. "In case I don't get a chance to say this later, it's been very good working with all of you."

"You'll have plenty of chances to talk all you want," the blonde told him as they began to move the bed. "You're just trying to guilt-trip us, Dr. Welles."

He looked at Peter as he was being pushed out of the room. "Damn, but these young ones are sharp," he pretended to lament.

"Hey, we all had a great teacher," the male nurse informed him, then pretended to level a critical look at him. "Now let's see if you can be a great patient."

Welles sighed and shook his head. "The demands never stop."

Peter walked behind the gurney as the nurses pushed it to the service elevators in the center of the hospital. He blocked the chief of surgery's words from his mind and focused only on one thing.

Saving the man's life.

Chapter Fifteen

The operation had been a complete success.

Lasting well into five hours, it had been as close to textbook perfect as anything he'd ever done.

Textbook perfect.

It was a term he'd heard the older surgeon use more than once over the years he'd worked under and then with the man. It had always been applied with praise at a job well done.

Peter cleared his throat, feeling as if he was going to choke as emotions crashed into one another, leaving him dazed, disoriented.

Textbook perfect.

Except that the patient had died.

Not because of anything he, as Harry's neurosurgeon, had or hadn't done. He shoved his fisted hands deep into his pockets, fighting the assault of helplessness he felt. The blame wasn't with him, wasn't with anyone, really. But it didn't change the way he felt.

Lost. Cheated. And so damn angry he thought he was going to explode.

It seemed to have been going so well. The conditions were as good as they got. In a way, it had been almost an easier surgery than he'd been braced for. Moving carefully, he had managed to get at the aneurysm that could have ended Harry Welles's life at any moment and had excised it with all the skill and precision that his years of surgery had enabled him to develop.

Not a thing had gone wrong then.

It was after the incision had been sewn up and his part in saving Harry's life had been completed that the crisis had occurred. As the chief of surgery was being brought up from under the anesthetic, Harry's blood pressure, which had been borderline but never dangerous all of his adult life, had suddenly spiked. It brought on a seizure, and then the man's heart had stopped.

They'd gone into code blue measures immediately. It was all a blur now, details melding together in his brain. The battle had been endless.

Eternal.

And futile.

All tolled, he'd fought for over forty-eight minutes, refusing to give in, refusing to listen to the death knell rendered by the monitor that showed Harry flat-lining. He absolutely refused to believed that someone as vital, as influential, as Harry could just be there one moment and not the next. Not when the operation was a success.

In the end, all his measures to save the chief of surgery were to no avail. Harry was gone. Not because of him, but on his watch.

The pain was overwhelming.

The knocking that echoed within the room mimicked it.

Peter wasn't even sure how he had gotten from the operating room down to his first-floor office. He remembered pushing past Raffety, the assistant surgeon, snapping at the nurse who tried to say something to him and the next thing he was really aware of, he was standing here, staring out the window. Seeing the sun shining and wondering how that was possible on a day like today.

Whoever was knocking on his door refused to stop. Instead, the noise became louder. It got to the point where he couldn't ignore it any longer.

"Go away," he growled, not even bothering to turn around so his voice could carry better.

Finally, the knocking stopped. He saw the door

being opened in the window's reflection. It gave his anger somewhere to go.

"Damn it," he shouted, finally turning around, "I said go away." And then he stopped, caught off guard. Raven stood in the doorway, her hand resting on the doorknob. He struggled to rein in his anger. "Now isn't a good time, Raven," he told her woodenly.

"I know." Her voice was soft, gentle. Raven closed the door behind her and crossed to him. "George called me."

It took him a second to process the words. It wasn't easy. Like the aftermath of a devastating forest fire, his mind felt burned out and in ruins. "I don't understand. Why would Grissom call you?"

She touched his arm. He felt stiff, like a mere statue of the man she'd fallen in love with. "Because he's worried. Because no one else, including him, has the nerve to approach you." She paused, her eyes never leaving his face. With all her heart, she wanted to be able to reach him. To lift the burden he'd so obviously slid onto his shoulders. "He told me what happened."

"He told you I killed Harry?" Peter sincerely doubted it. The hospital administrator was nothing if not careful with his wording. But that was exactly what he'd done. Killed Harry.

Peter sighed. He hadn't even discussed the surgery with her, trying very hard to keep the lines between his professional and private life drawn and clear. Not that there had been very much of the latter until Raven had waltzed into it. But the more time he spent with her, around her, the more blurred the lines became.

And they shouldn't be, he silently insisted. Moreover, he didn't deserve the compassion he saw in her eyes, either.

Raven tried to touch him, but he pulled back. "You didn't kill anyone," she insisted.

He laughed dryly, shaking his head. "You weren't there."

Though everything in his manner told her to, she wasn't about to back away. "George said that you had closed up, that you'd gotten the aneurysm. Peter, you did your best."

Peter shrugged carelessly. "My best wasn't good enough."

He couldn't really believe that, she thought. They both knew he was the best in his field. "Yes, it was. No one could have foreseen what happened."

He looked at her, angry at Raven for trying to make him feel better. A great man had died on the table after he'd operated on him. He didn't *want* to feel better, didn't deserve to feel better.

"I should have," he snapped at her, turning away.

Moving, she got in front of Peter, forcing him to look at her. "Why? Are you God?"

For a second, as the question echoed in his head, a strange smile played on his lips. "Funny, that was the first thing Blue ever said to me," he remembered. "Your brother looked into my office and asked me if I was God."

"Well, you're not, you know." Her voice was both firm and understanding at the same time. He wondered how she managed to pull that off. "What you do in that operating room is perform little miracles, but it doesn't make you God."

There wasn't anything she could say to make him feel better about what had happened. Why hadn't he reviewed the pre-op history and physical more closely? Why hadn't his mind flagged the fact that Harry's blood pressure was just at the acceptable limit?

He tried very hard to hold on to his temper, which was shredding right in front of him. "Look, I appreciate what you're trying to do, but just go."

He nodded toward the door, but Raven didn't budge. She didn't want to leave him, not when he was so bent on blaming himself. "I don't think you should be alone at a time like this."

And then his temper snapped. It was almost as if he was standing apart, watching himself shout at Raven. "What you think doesn't matter. I want to be alone, understand? I *am* alone."

She took a deep breath, her eyes never wavering from his face. He couldn't tell what she was thinking and part of him was ashamed for the way he was behaving. But he couldn't help himself and understanding was the last thing he wanted right now.

"All right," Raven told him quietly, "I'll go. But whether I leave this room or not, you are *not* alone. You never will be."

Turning on her heel, she crossed to the door and opened it, moving quickly so that he wouldn't see the tears gathering in her eyes. He'd turned away from her. She couldn't have him turning back because of guilt, because he'd seen the tears. She didn't want him that way. She wanted him turning toward her because he needed to. Because he needed her as much as she had come to realize that she needed him.

But it wasn't something she could make him see, or even wanted to make him see. This was something Peter had to figure out on his own.

And maybe he never would, she thought as she kept walking, trying hard not to give in to the overwhelming hurt that was growing inside her chest like a beast that required tribute.

Raven didn't cry until she got into her car.

The pounding woke her. It took her a second to orient herself. It was the sound of a fist beating against her front door.

She'd fallen asleep downstairs in the family room after putting Blue to bed. The boy had sensed that there was something wrong and asked her about it. She'd managed to put him off by saying she was just feeling under the weather. She didn't think Blue really bought the excuse, but, unusually sensitive to her feelings, he'd let it go for now, which was what she'd been hoping for. The boy was one in a million.

The pounding grew louder.

It was definitely coming from the front door. Connie was spending the night with a friend. Nerves began to stand on end, jumping around within her. There was no one else in the house except for her and Blue.

Scrambling to her feet, she immediately hurried to the closest phone to call the security company whose services she employed. The receiver was in her hand and she'd already pressed the automatic dial button when she heard Peter's voice.

"C'mon, Raven, open the door."

A deep male voice echoed from within the receiver. "Empire Security, how may I assist you?"

Peter? What was he doing here? Distracted, confused, she told the voice on the other end of the line, "Never mind. False alarm." Replacing the receiver, she hurried to the front door. Even before she reached it, she called out his name. "Peter?"

"Yes, it's me. Open the door, Raven." And then he added, "Please," in a voice she'd never heard before.

Undoing the two locks on the front door, Raven opened it and stepped back. "Come in."

He looked awful, she thought. Like a man who had spent the last few hours fighting demons for the ownership of his soul. Since he was here, she assumed that he had won. But the look in his eyes gave her no clues. The term "dead man walking" whispered across her mind.

Peter said nothing as he walked in, looking neither left nor right. Steeling herself for whatever was coming, she moved in front of him and led the way to the family room.

Since Blue hadn't appeared at the top of the stairs, wanting to know what was happening, he hadn't woken the boy up. She was hoping to keep it that way. She wasn't sure that whatever Peter had to say to her could or should be witnessed by an eight-year-old.

Once they were inside the family room, she turned to look at him. "Can I get you anything? Coffee? Scotch? A hair shirt?" she couldn't help adding.

It took him another long moment before he said anything. "I'm an idiot."

Raven stared at him in amazement. "You certainly know how to throw someone a curve, don't you?"

The word "throw" made Peter wince. He had no idea how to make any of this up to her, only that he had to try. "I came to apologize for throwing you out of my office today."

They saw things differently, she thought. But then, she was beginning to think that it was in his nature to assume the blame. Heroes did that, put themselves in front so that the bullet got them first.

"You didn't throw me out, Peter," she reminded him. "I left voluntarily."

She was kind, he thought. That was inherently in her nature. "After I told you to."

She smiled then, looking up into his eyes. Silently asking him to stop blaming himself. "That's hardly throwing."

She was a mystery to him. "Why aren't you angry at me?"

"I think you're angry enough at yourself." There was compassion in every syllable and unlike earlier that day, he realized that he both needed and wanted her compassion. Because it made him whole. *She* made him whole. "I think you're feeling so many things right now that it scares you to pieces and all you can do is lash out."

She had his number. A protest automatically sprang to his lips, but he let it go. It would have been a lie anyway. Very slowly, he blew out a breath and then nodded. "That about covers it, I guess."

Raven pressed her lips together, holding her

breath. Watching him. ''So you're through?'' She asked.

He nodded. He wasn't accustomed to apologizing and had no idea how his apology had been received. Was she asking him to go? ''Do you want me to leave?''

''Not unless you want to.'' Holding perfectly still, resisting the impulse to throw herself into his arms, she looked up into his face, trying very hard to read it. ''Do you want to?''

''No. No,'' he repeated. ''I don't. I don't ever want to leave you.''

Again he'd thrown her a curve. Raven was afraid to think she'd heard what she believed he'd said. He was going to have to spell things out to her.

''What are you saying?''

Peter didn't answer her directly. Instead, for just a moment, he reflected on what had happened that morning. ''Funny how life can be. One second, the operation's over and we're congratulating ourselves on a job well done, the next, we're fighting to save that same man's life.''

He had no idea how to say any of this, except to just plow through it and hope that, in the end, it would make sense to her.

Looking for the inner strength that she seemed to possess, he took her hands in his. ''Harry opened up to me this morning. It was almost as if he knew he might not come out of it alive. He told me he thought of himself as a failure, a coward.''

''Dr. Welles?''

She'd only met the man that one time outside of Blue's operating room, but she knew that Harry Welles had been a highly respected surgeon, one of the top men in his field. Blair Memorial didn't appoint just anyone as their chief of surgery. The kind of reputation that Harry Welles had did not come easily.

Peter nodded. ''He said it was because he'd never had the nerve to risk having a wife and family of his own. He told me that he was afraid to get involved for the long haul.''

She understood what he was telling her. What Harry had been trying to tell Peter. ''Like you,'' she whispered.

''Not like me,'' he insisted, squeezing her hands. ''Not anymore. When you walked away today—''

''Was sent away,'' she corrected. But the corners of her mouth had lifted.

''By an idiot,'' he added.

Raven laughed softly, touching his face. There was love in every single movement. Even he was aware of it. Finally. ''Go on with your story.''

''When I told you to leave me alone—and you did—I thought that was going to be the last time I was ever going to see you.'' The look in her eyes told him he should have known better, but she said nothing, allowing him to continue. ''I started thinking about what my life would feel like without you.'' Damn, he wished he was better with words. It all sounded so inadequate. ''I didn't like it. Because it would be empty again, just as empty as it was when you first came into it.''

Needing to feel her against him, he pulled her into his arms. Relief flooded through him because he didn't detect even the slightest bit of resistance.

''I'm not sure how it happened, it certainly wasn't something I was conscious of, but I've fallen in love with you, Raven, and I don't want to lose you.'' Right now, he wanted to do nothing more in this world than kiss her, but he had to get this all out before his courage flagged again. ''I know there aren't any guarantees in life. I don't give them when I operate, I can't expect them when I live. There's just the moment we're in and I want to spend all the moments I have left to me with you.'' He took a breath as he entered the final leg of his entreaty. ''I know that this is sudden, Raven—''

''Sudden?'' Her eyes widened at the word. She laughed, shaking her head. ''I think I've been waiting to hear you say this ever since that very first morning in your office.''

He tried to determine if she was serious or just pulling his leg. ''Is this your psychic thing?''

''No, it's my 'woman's thing,''' Raven teased, remembering the same exchange, almost verbatim, between her parents. "Sometimes, a woman—a person," she corrected in silent tribute to her parents, "can just look at someone and know that they were meant to be together."

He found himself wanting to truly believe that. "I guess I'm a little slow when it comes to that."

"Doesn't matter if you're slow, as long as you eventually catch up." She threaded her arms around his neck, fitting her body against his. "Are we on the same page?"

God, she felt so good against him. As though she belonged. As though he belonged, as well. He'd finally found a place for himself in this world and it was beside her. "I don't know, are we? Does your page say that you love me?"

A laugh, soft, sexy, excited, bubbled up within her. "In big, fat, bold letters that even a nearsighted crow could read from fifty yards away."

Despite her teasing voice, there was a solemnity in her eyes that spoke to him. That assured him it was all true, all real. "I guess that's a yes."

"In every single way." She turned her face up to his, her invitation clear.

But instead of kissing her, he resisted, needed to have this all out before he allowed himself to celebrate. "Then while you're in an agreeable mood, I guess I'd better slip in my proposal."

She heard the words, but refused to take them at

face value. He had to be talking about something else. "What proposal?"

"Marriage proposal."

Had he gone too far? he wondered. God, but he hoped not. Until he'd said the words out loud, he hadn't realized the full extent of his feelings. Hadn't realized just how much he wanted her to marry him.

She stared at him, her mouth dropping open. "As in 'will you marry me?'"

His arms tightened around her. "Why, yes, I will. Thanks for asking."

Confusion made her feel as if her very brain was throbbing. Heaven knew that the rest of her was. "But I didn't—you—" And then she gave up. She was too happy to care about protocol. "Oh, hell, it doesn't matter who asked who, just as long as the answer's yes for both of us."

Even as he began to kiss her, her words sparked a thought. He knew how important the boy was to her. Just a little more than Blue was to him. "Do you think Blue'll mind me marrying you?"

"Mind?" she echoed with a laugh. She loved that he could be so intelligent and still so innocent. "What do you think my brother wished for when he blew out his birthday candles?"

"You're kidding."

She grinned, moving her head from side to side. "I have it on the very best authority. Now, correct me if I'm wrong, but aren't marriage proposals usually followed by something a little more physical?''

A little of the twinkle he'd seen in her eyes felt as if it had entered his soul. ''Want to play a game of touch football?'' he teased just before he pulled her as close to him as the laws of physics allowed.

She sighed softly, loving the feel of him. ''Maybe later.''

Peter lowered his mouth to hers. ''Sounds good to me,'' he told her just before he kissed her.

* * * * *

Don't miss Marie Ferrarella's next romance
from Silhouette Intimate Moments:
DANGEROUS DISGUISE
(IM1339)
Available January 2005